DRINKING WITH THE ENEMY

"Hey, pretty lady? Wan' have a drink with me?"

"Go away, Mister," Belle said. "If you know what's good for you, go away."

"He just wants to take you for a drink, Belle," Griff said.

"I don't drink with drunks."

That didn't stop Mason.

"Get away from me!" Belle yelled, and started to go for her gun.

"Don't!" Mason said. He dropped his drunk guise and brought his hand out from behind his back, where he'd been holding his gun. "Don't try it."

Belle froze. It took precious seconds for Griff to pull his attention away from the blood that was staining his pants and his boots, and by that time Clint had come out of the alley.

"Don't be foolish," he called to Griff.

Griff turned and saw Clint covering him.

"Who are you?"

"The man who's going to put you away . . ."

THE GUNSMITH

214

THE BORTON FAMILY GANG

J. R. ROBERTS

JOVE BOOKS, NEW YORK

This is a work of fiction. Names, characters, places, and incidents are
either the product of the author's imagination or are used fictitiously,
and any resemblance to actual persons, living or dead, business
establishments, events or locales is entirely coincidental.

THE BORTON FAMILY GANG

A Jove Book / published by arrangement with
the author

PRINTING HISTORY
Jove edition / October 1999

The Penguin Putnam Inc. World Wide Web site address is
http://www.penguinputnam.com

ISBN: 0-515-12661-6

A JOVE BOOK®
Jove Books are published by The Berkley Publishing Group,
a division of Penguin Putnam Inc.,
375 Hudson Street, New York, New York 10014.
JOVE and the "J" design
are trademarks belonging to Penguin Putnam Inc.

PRINTED IN THE UNITED STATES OF AMERICA

10 9 8 7 6 5 4 3 2 1

THE GUNSMITH

214

THE BORTON FAMILY GANG

ONE

There was no doubt about the fact that Belle Jackson, Barbara Anderson—who they called "Baby" because she was the youngest—and Kate Lawrence were wicked women. They were wicked because they wanted to be. They enjoyed it immensely. It made life interesting for them—just as riding with the Borton Gang did.

There were five Borton brothers, and the three women had to service all five. Not that they minded much. All three of them liked danger and sex, and they got both with the Bortons.

But the Bortons had gone into the town of Tierney, Arizona, and left the women in camp. They were going to scout out the bank and, eventually, rob it. It could take a day, or two, or three—and by day four the women were bored and ready for sex.

This was the state Clint Adams found them in when he rode up to their camp.

• • •

Clint came within sight of the camp and saw three women alone, with no men. This seemed odd to him. He wanted to stop and ask if they needed any help, but he didn't want to frighten them. He decided to dismount and walk Duke into the camp with his hands in plain sight.

As he approached the camp, he sized up all three women. They were of differing shapes; one was rather solidly built, but not unattractively so; one was very slender—but again, not unattractive—and the other was built somewhere in between. He couldn't see their faces yet, until suddenly the solid one turned and noticed him. She turned to face his head and said something to the other women.

"Stop right there," the solid one said, with her hands on her hips. She had big, solid breasts and hips and appeared to be in her late thirties. Her hair was once coal black, but now had some streaks of gray in it. Maybe she was older than he'd first surmised.

The other two women grabbed guns and pointed them at him. The slender one looked the youngest—maybe twenty—and blond, while the third one looked to be in her late twenties and was a redhead. However, they all looked about the same with the equalizers they were pointing.

"Excuse me, ladies," he said, "but I was just going to ask if you needed any help."

"Why would we need help from a stranger?" the solid one asked.

"I just thought, three women alone, you could use a hand."

"And maybe you were looking for a meal?" she asked.

"That'd be nice, Ma'am."

The woman studied him for a moment, sizing him up, then leaned over and said something to the other two, which they nodded their agreement to.

"All right, Mister," she said, "you can come ahead into camp. We don't need no help, but we don't turn away anybody who needs a meal."

"I'm much obliged for that, Ma'am," Clint said. "Could you, uh, have your two friends put those guns away."

"We'll put 'em away," the middle woman said, "but not too far."

"Fair enough," Clint said. "I'll just go and picket my horse with yours."

"Coffee'll be ready when you get back," the first woman said.

He walked Duke over to where their horses were tied. There were four of them—one obviously a pack animal—but he immediately noticed the tracks in the dirt, indicating that, at one time, there had been a lot more horses. Maybe he was wrong. Maybe they weren't alone, without any men.

He came back to the campfire and all three women seemed to be involved with the cooking. One was pouring coffee, one was stirring a big pot, and the other was slicing some wild onions.

"Can I help?" he asked.

"Just have a seat and some coffee," the first woman said, handing him a cup.

"Thank you, Ma'am—uh, can we exchange names,

so I don't have to keep calling you all 'Ma'am'?''

"I'm Belle," the first woman said, who then pointed to the middle one and added, "that's Kate."

"And you?" Clint asked the youngest one.

"Barbara," she said.

"We call her Baby," Belle said.

"I hate that name!"

"Well, that's what we call her," Belle said.

"My name is Clint," he said. "I couldn't help but notice the tracks on the ground over there. There are more of you?"

"Yes," Belle said.

"More women?"

"Men."

"Oh. Well, will they mind if they find me here? I don't want to get shot by a jealous husband."

"Husband?" Belle asked. "Ha! No husbands in that group, friend. And they won't be coming back anytime soon."

"Did you have a falling out?"

"Well, they are a bunch of unreasonable jerks," she said, "but now, they're just out . . . looking for ways to make money."

"I see."

Baby dropped the sliced onions into the pot that Kate was stirring.

"That smells real good."

"Trail stew," Belle said.

"Sounds like you've cooked for cowboys in your past," Clint said.

"Mister," Belle said, "I done just about everything in my past."

Looking at the big, sturdily built woman, Clint could believe it.

TWO

The coffee was good, strong trail coffee, and the stew was excellent. Clint contributed some dry biscuits to the feast, and they all ate heartily.

He studied each of the women in turn while they ate.

Belle was the leader, both mother and caretaker. She made sure everyone had enough to eat and rarely took her eyes off of Clint, still not quite trusting him. When she leaned forward to fill his plate again, her breasts swelled and threatened to overflow from the top of her dress. Clint found his eyes drawn there, then to her eyes, where he saw no disapproval. Apparently, she was used to men looking down the neck of her dress.

Kate was wearing a shirt and skirt, and the skirt was belted tight at the waist. The shirt emphasized her breasts which—while not as big as Belle's—were full and round.

Barbara—or "Baby"—could have put her hair in pigtails and passed for fourteen, but with her hair down

6

and wearing a woman's dress, she had all the appeal of a woman. Her breasts were as small and hard as peaches and were bare beneath the cloth of her taffeta dress.

Undeniably, all of these women were attractive. Clint couldn't help wondering what they were doing out here, alone, and what it was their men did to earn their money.

He had an idea, but it was probably unfair of him to assume that their men were outlaws—that would make them outlaw's women and, if that was the case, he ought to mount up and put as much space between himself and them as possible before their men came back.

But Belle had assured him that they wouldn't be back anytime soon, and he and Duke did need to rest. Also, the hot food had a lot to do with his ultimate decision to stay.

After they ate he offered to help with the dishes. "Woman's work," Belle told him firmly, and the task fell to Barbara.

Belle poured him another cup of coffee and told him to keep out of the way. He took his coffee to a rock on the other side of camp and watched as they scurried around, working together as a team. These three women had been traveling together for quite a while.

Kate came up to him, finally, and looked into his half-filled cup.

"That must be cold by now," she said. "We're makin' another pot. I'll bring you some."

"Sure," he said. "Thanks, Kate."

She walked to the fire, poured him a fresh cup and brought it back to him.

"Thank you," he said, again.

She started away but he grabbed her wrist, gently, but firmly.

"Why don't you sit with me?" he asked.

"I got chores," she said. "Belle wouldn't like it."

"Is Belle the boss?"

"Not the boss," she said. "She's just, sort of, in charge until—"

"Until what?"

"Nothin'."

"Until the men come back?"

She nodded.

"And when would that be?"

"Not for a few days, at least."

"Why would they leave you alone out here for that long?" he asked.

"We're not helpless."

"No, you're not," he said. "I saw that as soon as I walked in. Still, I don't think I'd leave three lovely ladies alone on the trail."

She touched her hair at the compliment, then said, "—I got to take care of those chores."

"Sure," he said, "I understand," and he released her wrist. She hesitated a moment, as if there was something else she wanted to say, then turned and walked back to the area around the camp fire.

Moments later Belle was walking toward him, and he braced himself.

THREE

"The girls like you," she said.

"Does that mean you don't?"

"I'm more careful than they are."

"Would you like me to leave?"

She folded her arms beneath her ample breasts and asked, "If I said yes, would you?"

"Yes."

"Without a fuss?"

"Why not?" he asked. "I've already gotten more than I bargained for."

She studied him for a few moments, then said, "You can bed down on this side of the fire. We'll be on the other side."

"Will you be setting a watch?"

"No need," she said. "If anyone else comes riding in we know who it'll be."

Clint didn't find that remark very comforting.

"But don't look so worried," she said. "The men

9

won't be back for some time. We have all the time in the world."

As she walked away he wondered what she meant by that remark.

Clint checked Duke one last time before turning in. He bade all three women good night, rolled himself up in his blanket, and went to sleep.

He was awakened sometime later by someone nudging him, poking his shoulder.

"Hey," a voice whispered.

"Hmm?"

Another nudge.

"What?"

"Shhh," she said, "keep your voice down."

He rolled over and looked at the woman who was nudging him. It was Belle, and she was standing above him, totally naked. She was, indeed, a big, solidly built woman, with breasts like melons, heaving thighs and—he knew without looking—a fine, big butt. Between her legs there was a wild tangle of black hair, and that's where he found himself staring.

"I ain't had a man in a week," she said. "That's too long for me. You interested?"

He hesitated only a moment, then tossed back his blanket. She crawled on top of him, almost smothering him with her large, firm breasts. He took them in his hands and began to kiss them, sucking the nipples, then biting them. Her hand slid down to undo his trousers and slide inside. When she found him he was already hard.

"Ooh, yeah," she said, "you got a nice one, all right. I knew you would."

She was lit only by moonlight, but it seemed to him that acres of flesh were above him, and he had no complaint. She smelled good, her skin was as smooth as a baby's, and he could smell her sex, all wet and waiting.

"Let me help you," she said, grasping his trousers and pulling them down to his boots, along with his underwear. Now, by the light of the moon, she looked at him, and she obviously liked what she saw.

"God, you're a pretty man," she said. "That's the prettiest damn cock I ever saw."

"Thank you," he said, "you're not so bad yourself."

"Oh, hell, I know I ain't pretty," she said. "I'm too fat to be pretty, but I ain't too fat to be good at this—and I am."

"I'm sure you are."

"Well," she said, "maybe you're sure, but I'm gonna show ya, anyway."

She unbuttoned his shirt and helped him get it off, then ran her hands over his chest. Her hands were probably the only part of her that wasn't soft, but they'd no doubt been hardened by hard work, and that was nothing to be ashamed of.

He pulled her down so that she was lying on him and began to kiss her shoulders and her neck. At the same time his hands roamed over her, touching, rubbing, kneading . . .

"Good Lord, Mister," she said is hushed tones, "what're you doin' to me?"

"I'm trying to make you feel good," he said into her ear. "Just relax and enjoy it."

With that he turned her over onto her back, then got to his knees and looked down at her. In the moonlight her distended nipples looked almost black. He leaned over and began to kiss and suck her breasts in earnest. They were among the most beautiful breasts he had ever seen, full, firm, smooth, her nipples sensitive—so sensitive that she shuddered and sighed through several small orgasms. She sighed and held his head as he ran his mouth over her, and then he began to take his mouth lower, kissing the little extra roll of flesh around her waist, going lower still until his tongue was probing her public thatch. She was gasping, bucking her hips as if she was actually riding his tongue . . .

"God . . . God . . . ooooh, God," she said, the last coming out gutteral, like a cry. "Jesus . . . I'm gonna die . . ."

He stopped what he was doing and looked up at her.

"You're not going to die, Belle," he said. "You're going to feel very alive."

He went back to work on her with his mouth again, and before long her body was as taut as a bow string . . . and then she exploded, almost flopping about uncontrollably until he raised himself over her and plunged his rigid penis into her again and again. She lifted her hips to him each time he came down, and he slid his hands beneath her glorious buttocks and fucked her harder and harder until she exploded yet again . . .

"I'm nigh onto forty years old and I ain't *never* felt anything like that in my life," she said, a little later.

"Then men haven't been treating you right, Belle."

They were lying together, and now she stood up and stared down at him.

"You're a dangerous man, Clint."

"How's that?"

"You could make a woman doubt herself."

"You've got no reason to doubt yourself, Belle. You were wonderful."

"I ain't talkin' about sex," she said. She stood up abruptly. "I got to get back before the girls wake and miss me."

"If you weren't talkin about sex, what were you talking about?"

"Everything," she said, "just everything."

FOUR

He fell back to sleep only to be awakened again by a nudge. Belle again?

"Hey!" a woman said.

"Hmm?"

He rolled over, expecting to see Belle again, but it wasn't Belle, it was the young one, the one they called "Baby." She wasn't naked, as Belle had been, so her intentions were not as immediately evident.

"Barbara? What is it? Is something wrong?" he asked her.

"Yeah," she said, "somethin' is real wrong. I got me an itch that ain't been scratched in a week—if you know what I mean."

Clint had no idea what time it was, or how much time had gone by since he'd been with Belle. Barbara got on her knees and began to unbutton her dress. In seconds, her breasts, small but round, spilled out as she pulled the dress down over her shoulders. Before long she was

14

naked from the waist up, her belly button a shadowy mystery in the moonlight.

"Do you think I'm pretty?" she asked.

"I think you're very pretty, Barbara," he said, reaching out to stroke her breasts, "I think you're very pretty."

As he touched her breasts, her nipples came to life and she gasped and bit her bottom lip. They soon managed to remove her dress completely, and he was once again naked that night.

They rolled onto the blanket together. This one was insistent and didn't want to wait long. She was immediately wet and reached down to grab his penis and shove it inside her. She was on top of him, sitting up straight and riding up and down on him. He reached up to palm her small breasts and pop the nipples between his fingers while she bounced up and down on him.

"God," she said, "it feels like you're right . . . here," and she touched herself between her breasts. That was all she said. He didn't know how much time passed, but it seemed as if she rode him forever, tossing her head back, biting her lower lip, saying, "Just a little more . . . just a little more . . ." He bit his own lip, trying to stay with her, and when her time came she shuddered and whimpered, and he stopped fighting it and ejaculated with almost painful urgency. She fell on him, breathing hard.

"I ain't never had a man stay inside me this long," she said, because he was still in her and still semi-erect.

"Why not?"

"Most men just want to get it over with for their own pleasure, you know?"

"Well then, most men are selfish, aren't they?"

"Well, yes," she said, "they're men."

"Right."

They lay there like that for a while, and then she sat up and got off of him, his partially erect penis sliding out of her.

"Did you . . . I mean, I hope you . . . did you?"

He smiled and said, "I did."

"But you're still . . . big."

"That's because you're so pretty."

She reached out and stroked his testicles and penis, which swelled to its full size.

"God, I'd like to stay but I got to go before the others know I'm gone."

She stood up and pulled on her dress, then impulsively leaned over him and kissed him. He realized it was the first kiss they'd had.

" 'Night," she said, and hurried away.

Clint was so tired he didn't even bother to get dressed. He just wrapped himself in his blanket and went to sleep.

FIVE

It felt to Clint as if he had barely fallen back to sleep when someone nudged his shoulder. He rolled over and was not surprised to see Kate standing there.

"We drew straws," she said, "and I got to go last. I hope you're not too tired?"

She unbuttoned her shirt and removed it, revealing breathtakingly beautiful breasts, with just a sprinkling of freckles between them. When she kicked off her skirt he realized that, of the three, she had the most beautiful body. Belle's breasts might have been a little bigger, and Barbara's skin might have been smoother, but Kate won the prize, hands down, for overall beauty.

She reached up behind her head to release her hair from its tie and the movement made her breasts stand out. He noticed that her nipples were already erect. He wondered if things had gone even further than drawing straws? Were the women comparing his performance?

Was Kate already excited because she had heard about what he did with Belle and Barbara?

Clint was surprised at his own vigor as he welcomed Kate to his blanket. He was anxious to be with her, and his erect penis was evidence of this. She grasped it lightly and ran her nail up and down the underside of him, sending delicious sensations throughout his body. He had the feeling that, of the three women, Kate was the most sexually experienced. For her age, Belle had been surprisingly unimaginative—not that he hadn't enjoyed himself with her, because he had—and Barbara had been almost shy. Kate began to kiss his chest and tossed the blanket back even further so that his erection was in plain sight. She kissed her way down his chest and belly until she was nose-to-head with him, and then she began to lick him. He lifted his hips as she ran her tongue up and down him, and then she swooped down and took him into her mouth. She sucked him wetly, holding the base of his penis with the thumb and forefinger of her right hand, fondling his testicles with her left, then running her hands up and down his thighs and finally sliding her hands beneath him to cup his buttocks.

Clint had no idea they were being watched.

He had no idea of anything but her mouth . . .

"My God," Barbara said to Belle as they watched from a hiding place, "how can she take that whole thing in her mouth?"

"Kate's got some talents you don't know about, Baby," Belle said.

"Have you ever done that, Belle?"

"No," she said, "I can't say that I have—but I'm looking forward to it."

"Which of the brothers are you gonna do it to?" Barbara asked.

"Them? I wouldn't put one of them in my mouth in a bet," Belle said with a disgusted look. "Not unless he come right from a bath—and you know what the chances of that are."

"None."

"Right. No, I'm gonna do it with our friend Clint, here."

"God," Barbara said, as she was unable to take her eyes off of the two undulating bodies on the blanket, "I wish I had a body like Kate's."

"Yeah," Belle said, feeling like a horse standing next to little Baby, "she sure has a perfect little ass on her, don't she . . . the bitch?"

Kate released Clint's penis from her mouth and was now presenting him with her perfect little ass. He got behind her, grasped her hips and slid his wet penis right into her from the back. She bucked against him, and clenched her butt cheeks on him, as if she was trying to yank his seed from him.

Clint moved with her, reached around in front of her to touch her, her breasts, her nipples, her belly, lower still until his fingers were moist with her juices and she was gasping for breath . . . and then suddenly she went wild and he had to hold on. As waves of pleasure flowed over her, she clenched and unclenched and suddenly he was exploding into her, ejaculating for the third time that night and, amazingly, probably harder than before . . .

• • •

"I have to get back . . ." she said, starting to leave the blanket.

"Why?" he asked. "You're not going to tell me you have to get back before the others see you're gone."

"Well . . ."

"Unless I miss my bet," he said, "they've been watching us the whole time."

"Well . . ."

"And I think it's about time one of you stayed with me and kept me warm."

She seemed to consider it, lying there with her butt against his belly. His penis was swelling, seemed to be crawling up her ass, which surprised both of them.

"Well, all right," she said, drawing the blanket back over them, "just to keep you warm . . ."

SIX

When morning came, Kate was still in the blankets with Clint, and they were both still naked. Nobody had come to wake them, which was good. It meant that the men hadn't returned during the night, and Belle and Barbara weren't too angry about Kate staying with him. If they were, they would have delighted in waking them.

Kate was lying with her back to him, so he leaned over and kissed her neck.

"Time to get up."

"Mmmm," she said, reaching behind her for his penis.

"Oh no, you don't," he said, slapping her hand away, "you want to kill me?"

"I want more, Clint," she said. "You owe me, I stayed the night."

"Okay, relax," he said, and pressed up against the back of her. He ran his hand over her breasts and nipples, kissing the back of her shoulders. His hand traced

21

the smooth skin down over her belly and into the patch of red hair that was not as wild as Belle's black bush. He began to stroke her with his fingers, getting her wet, sliding one finger into her and kept it up until she was biting her lips to keep from crying out . . .

"That what you had in mind?" he asked, moments later.

"Oh, my God," she said, gasping. "You did it with . . . your hand?"

"Nobody's ever done that for you before?"

"No man has ever done nothin' for me," she said. "It's always the other way around. Can you do that again?"

"Well, if we've got time—"

"No," she said, "I meant, can you do that . . . every time?"

"Well, that depends on the woman and how sensitive she is."

"God," she said, again, "you're a dangerous man, Clint."

"That's funny," he said, "that's what Belle said, too."

She rolled out of the blankets and pulled on her skirt and shirt.

"I got to help get breakfast," she said.

"Good," he said, "I've built up an appetite."

And as she hustled away he added to himself, *And I didn't get much sleep.*

SEVEN

By the time Clint made his way to the campfire, all of the women were up and dressed and doing their share of the chores. None of them brought up what took place during the night, and that was fine with him, because for it to have happened these women had to be very close— almost like family. If that was the case, he wanted to have some coffee, have something to eat, and then hit the trail before the rest of the "family" showed up.

The only concession the women seemed to have made to what happened during the night was the clothing they were wearing, which were cleaner and better than what they'd been wearing when he first arrived. Also, they seemed to have bathed, so there must have been a creek or something nearby. Belle was the only one dressed suggestively, wearing something that was almost a peasant blouse, really showing off the slopes of her big breasts.

"Coffee?" Belle asked.

"Yes, please."

She poured a cup and handed it to him.

"Flapjacks'll be ready in a minute or two," Barbara said.

"Good," he answered. "I'm starved."

"I'll check on the horses," Kate said.

"Don't get too close to mine," he called after her. "He might take off a finger."

"I can handle horses," she called over her shoulder to him.

"I'm just warning you . . ." he called back.

"She's really good with horses," Belle said. "Mine's getting even more ornery around strangers in his old age."

"What do you want to bet she wins him over?" Belle asked.

"What are the stakes?"

Belle and Barbara exchanged a glance. They'd been discussing earlier how to get Clint to stay another day—and night. They figured that would be cutting it close enough to when the men were supposed to come back.

"If you lose," Belle said, "you stay another night."

He smiled.

"And if I win?"

"You get whichever of us you want."

"Wait a minute," Clint said. "Let me get this straight. If I win, I get one of you tonight, and if I lose I get all three of you? That's losing?"

"Sounds like a good deal to me," Belle said.

"Almost too good," he said. "I think I'll pass on the bet. If I win, Kate will be minus at least one finger."

"But will you stay?" Barbara asked. "One more night?"

He'd already decided that he was leaving after breakfast, and he wanted to stick to that decision.

"Barbara, I'd like to, but I've got to get going," he said. "You three ladies have been . . . well, an experience I won't soon forget. Besides, won't your men be coming back soon?"

"Them!" Barbara said. "They don't know how to satisfy a woman the way you do."

"Amen," Belle said.

"I'm sorry as hell about that," Clint said, accepting a plate from Barbara, "but I really do have to be going."

"Well," Belle said, "if you have to, you have to."

"I do."

"Eat up, then," she said. "we can't have you leaving on an empty stomach."

Barbara gave Belle a look like she was crazy and pulled her aside.

"We can't let him go," she said, urgently. "Not without one more night."

"I know," Belle said. "I have a plan."

"What is it?"

Belle told her, and Barbara smiled.

EIGHT

There were five Borton brothers, and they were all standing outside the Bank of Tierney. They weren't together, though. Ted Borton was sitting across the street in a wooden chair, because he was the lookout. Ben and Griff Borton were going to go into the bank first, and then Jake would go in. Lastly, Will, the youngest, would stay outside with the horses.

Will didn't like the idea of being left out and argued about it the night before, but Ben told him somebody had to watch the horses.

"We don't want another Northfield," Ben, the oldest, said, referring to the James/Younger Gang's debacle in Minnesota about a year before.

"What did that have to do with horses?" Will demanded.

"It has to do with doing what you're told, Will," Ben said. "Now just do it."

"When do I get to go into a bank?" Will demanded.

"Soon," his oldest brother told him.

Now it was morning, and the bank was just about to open. Ben had watched and waited and had finally figured that this was the best time of day to pull the job. The sheriff, even if he was awake, would still be groggy from a night's sleep and would be slow to respond even if some shots were fired.

All the brothers had orders, though. No shooting unless somebody else shot first.

"Why we got to worry about killing anybody?" Griff asked. "We done it before." And Griff *enjoyed* every minute of it.

"Just take it easy, Griff," Ben said. "Don't go off half-cocked like—"

He stopped, but it was too late.

"Like what?" Griff demanded. "Like that time in Abilene? Is that what you was gonna say. Jesus Christ, I shoot a couple of lawmen one time and I can never live it down?"

"That posse chased us for months, Griff," Ben said. "If we hadn't split up they woulda caught us."

"So what?" Griff asked. "We got back together again, didn't we?"

"Yeah, we did," Ben said, "and you agreed to do what I told you. Remember that?"

Griff fumed and said, "Okay, after this job maybe we ought to renegotiate."

"You want to be the leader of this family, this gang, Griff?" Ben asked. "Be my guest."

Ben had kept Griff with him because the middle brother of the five had a habit of getting impatient and using his gun. Ben was in favor of getting in and out clean, and leaving no mess behind. When it was just money involved, posses gave up easier.

Now he and Griff crossed the street as they saw the shades on the bank doors roll up.

"Open for business," Griff said.

"Yeah," Ben said, "our business."

They entered the bank and looked around. There were three bank tellers and another man who had unlocked the door.

"Oh," the man said, "you must have been waiting, gentlemen."

"Just a few minutes," Ben said.

"Well," the fussy-looking little man said, "my name is Horace Gateway, and I'm the bank manager. If you have any problems, please let me know."

"Don't worry, we will," Griff said.

Gateway nodded and went into his office, closing the door behind him.

"Let's do it," Griff said. "There's no customers."

"We're waiting for Jake."

"We can do this ourselves, Ben."

"Jake," Ben said.

Griff looked over at the tellers, one of which was a pretty young women. Griff missed their three women, but would have traded any of them for this pretty little filly. Well, maybe not Kate, but the other two were either too big for him or too small.

This one was just right.

"I miss the women," Ted said to Jake and Will.

"Me, too," Will said, "especially Baby."

"You were in the whorehouse last night, Will," Jake pointed out.

"And I picked me out a gal who reminded me of Baby," Will said, not bothering to deny it.

"Time to go," Jake said. "You remember what to do, Will?"

"Sure," Will said. "How hard can it be to hold the horses?"

"Ted?"

"I'm set."

Jake, the second oldest, said, "Then come on, youngster."

Griff was trying to talk to the lady teller when the door opened and Jake came in. There were still no other customers.

"Okay, Griff," Ben said, and they all drew their guns and pointed them at the tellers.

"Oh, no," the woman gasped—and then she gasped again when Griff reached through the teller's cage and grabbed her by the arm.

"You be nice to me, Missy, and maybe I'll take you with me when we leave."

"No!" she said, frightened.

"Let her go, Griff," Ben said. "That's not what we're here for."

Grudgingly, Griff released her.

"Who's head teller?" Ben asked.

"I am," a man said. He looked almost identical to the bank manager.

"You and that manager related?"

The man nodded. "He's my brother."

"He's manager and you're head teller? You happy with that?"

"That's how it worked out."

"Well," Ben said, "after we rob you maybe he'll get fired and you'll get his job."

"R-rob us?"

"What did you think this was?" Jake asked. "A birthday party? Start loading the money into some sacks."

"We don't have any s-sacks," the man said.

Griff cocked the hammer back on his gun, a sound that made the young woman jump, and said, "Find some, or she gets it first."

"And then you," Jake added.

"A-all right," the man said. "Sally, Joe, do as they say."

"What about the safe, friend?" Ben asked. "Can you open it?"

"No."

"Who can."

"Nobod—"

"If you lie to me, I'll know it, and I'll make you sorry. Who can open it?"

The man looked as if he was going to resist, but finally gave in.

"My brother."

"Get him."

"What do I tell him?"

"Tell him there's somebody out here who will only do business with him."

The teller, Samuel Gateway, walked to his brother's door and knocked.

NINE

Clint finished his breakfast and accepted another cup of coffee from Belle. He looked for Barbara and Kate and saw that they were off to one side, having a heated discussion about something. Maybe Baby was upset over Kate spending the night with Clint.

Belle was oddly quiet while he finished his last cup of coffee.

"Aren't you going to eat?" he asked.

"I never eat breakfast," she said. "I get any bigger nobody'll want me."

"I don't think that's true."

"I do," she said. "Men want girls like Kate, or even Baby. Not me."

"Belle, last night—"

"Last night you gave in three times to three different women, of different sizes and shapes. It wasn't *me* you wanted."

31

"It was," he said, "at that very moment when you appeared."

"And was it Baby and Kate you wanted when they appeared?"

"Of course."

"So then why do you want to leave so soon?" she asked him.

"Two reasons," he said. "One, I have someplace to go, and two, I don't think I should be here when your men come back."

"You afraid?"

"Damn right," he said, "afraid I might have to kill someone unnecessarily."

"There's five of them."

"I'd rather not face five men," he said, "but if I did, I'd take some of them with me."

"You're pretty confident."

"I just know what I can do."

She stared at him then and said, "Clint . . . Clint . . . and a big black horse."

He knew she was figuring it out.

"Say," she said, finally, "what's your last name?"

"Adams."

"You mean we all had sex with the Gunsmith?"

"I'm afraid so."

"Well," she said, "whataya think of that."

When the manager came out in reply to his brother's call, Ben Borton stuck his gun in the man's ear.

"Oh, dear," Horace Gateway said, and fainted.

"Damn it!" Ben swore as the man slumped to the

floor. "You!" He pointed to Samuel Gateway. "Wake him up, and make it quick."

While Sam Gateway tried to rouse his brother, Ben went over to stand next to Jake.

"This is taking too long. A customer is bound to show up."

"So let's just take what the tellers have and git," Jake said.

"There's a lot more in that safe," Ben said. "I *know* it."

"Ben," Jake said, "you don't want to have to—"

At that point the door opened and a man and a woman entered. The man was looking behind him, at Will Borton, who was holding onto five horses.

"Wonder what's going—" he started to say to the woman, but then he saw the armed gunmen.

The man looked unarmed, as he was without a holster. Ben relaxed for a moment, figuring they'd put these two up against a wall. However, the man had a gun tucked into his belt behind his back and he went for it.

"Jesse, no!" his wife yelled.

It was too late. He was bringing the gun around and when Jake Borton saw it he fired once, killing the man instantly.

"Oh, God, no! No!" his wife shouted.

Griff turned and shot her once in the head.

"What'd you do that for?" Ben asked.

"To shut her up," Griff said. "We don't need her screaming in here."

"We got to get out of here," Ben said, "and now. Griff, Jake, grab the bags. I'll check the street."

Ben went to the door and looked out. He saw Ted

running across the street to see what the shooting was about. Will was fighting the horses, which were skittish.

It was going wrong, Northfield all over again.

"No, no!"

Ben heard the woman and turned to see Griff tugging the female teller along with him.

"Please, don't take me," she cried.

"Griff!"

The two brothers locked eyes.

"Leave her be."

"I want her."

"She'll slow us down."

"Don't wait for me, then," Griff said. "I want her, I tell you."

Ben pointed his gun at his brother.

"You get one, Griff," he said, "the girl or your share of the money."

"You'd cheat me out of my share?"

"It's not cheating," Ben said. "You get to pick."

The door opened then and Ted stuck his head in, saw the bodies of the man and woman on the floor and quickly assessed the situation.

"We gotta get going," he called. "People are startin' to show up."

"Griff?" Ben said.

Griff roughly pushed the woman away from him, so that she almost fell.

"She ain't worth the money. Let's get out of here."

They went out of the bank with money bags in one hand and their guns in the other.

TEN

Clint was getting ready to saddle Duke when Kate came walking over to him, got in front of him, and started to pet Duke's nose. The big gelding suffered her touch without a hint of teeth gnashing.

"You old flirt," Clint said to him.

"We made friends this morning," she said.

"Well, I guess it's a good thing I didn't take Belle's bet."

"If you had," she asked, "and you'd won, which one of us would you have picked?"

"But I didn't bet and I didn't win, so I'm not going to answer that question."

"Take me with you," Kate said.

"Kate, I can't—"

"All right," she said, "just let me ride with you until we get to a town."

He looked at her. If he took her with him—if he *let* her ride with him—he was asking for trouble. Chances

35

were, whoever the men were who these women were riding with, they'd come looking for what they thought was theirs.

"Are you afraid?" she asked.

"Of five men? Yes, some."

"Belle told me who you are," she said. "Once they know that, they won't come after us."

He remained silent, thinking.

"Clint, I need to get away from them," she said. "They're the Borton brothers."

"The bank robbers?" he asked. "The ones who say they're better—or worse—than the James Boys?"

"That's right."

Now he knew they'd come after them, and wouldn't stop until they found her.

"Kate, I think you're better off here," he said.

"They have sex with me," she said, "all of them. Ben, the oldest, he also has sex with Belle, and then Griff and Will have sex with Baby, but *all* of them have sex with me—sometimes in one night."

He winced. It sounded painful to him.

"As soon as they get here," she said, "they'll put me on my back and get in line. I can't go through that anymore."

"All right," he said. "Get your horse saddled so we can get moving."

"Nobody's going noplace," Belle said from behind them.

They both turned and saw that Belle and Baby had them covered with their revolvers.

"Belle," Kate said, "we can all leave, together."

"Forget it."

"Baby?"

"I'm staying with Belle."

"But why?" Kate demanded. "Why stay when they treat us so badly."

"Speak for yourself," Belle said. "I been with Ben Borton a long time. We raised Baby, here."

Kate had always wondered why Ben never had sex with Baby. Could he really be her father, or had he and Belle simply raised her?

"Belle," Kate said, "let me go. You're jealous of me, I know it."

"I'm jealous of your youth and your beauty," Belle said, "but if I let you go, Ben will kill me." She gestured to Clint. "Drop your gunbelt. Unbuckle it left-handed and drop it."

"Belle," Clint said, "you're making a mistake. Men like the Bortons—"

"What do you know about them?"

"I guess I don't know anything about them, really," he said, unbuckling his belt, "except what I've heard about Ben, but I know about men just like them."

"You don't know nothin'," she said. "Oh, you know how to please a woman, all right, but you don't know nothin' about us if you think I'd leave now, with all this time invested."

"Invested?" Kate said. "Time wasted, is much more like it."

"You shut up, Kate," Belle said. "You're lucky I don't shoot you where you stand."

"Have you ever shot anyone, Belle?" Clint asked.

"Sure I have."

"Up close, like this? When you can see my face, my eyes? Baby, you ever shoot anyone?"

Looking scared, Baby shook her head.

"Well," Belle said, "today's a good day for her to start. You drop that gun belt, and if you try to whip it this way, I'll put a bullet in you."

"Why, Belle?" he asked. "Why keep me here?"

"The boys won't be back until tomorrow," Belle said. "We get one more night with you."

"I'm a prisoner and you expect me to perform?"

"You better," she said. "If you don't, I won't let you go tomorrow. I'll keep you here until the boys get back. They'll be real interested in the Gunsmith, oh yes they will."

"Belle—"

"I told you to shut up, Kate."

"Will she shoot me, Kate?" Clint asked.

"Oh yes," Kate said, "she'd shoot you in a second, Clint."

Clint nodded, and hesitated only a moment before he dropped his gun belt to the ground.

ELEVEN

The Bortons barely got out of Tierney with their lives. As they came out of the bank, someone started shooting at them. Ben saw a man with a badge standing in the street, firing. He fired once and the man went down. But by then the townspeople had taken up guns and were firing at them.

"Get mounted!" he shouted. "Get out of here!"

The brothers collected their horses from Will and swung into their saddles. As young Will swung up, a bullet hit him in the right shoulder from behind.

"Ben!" he shouted.

Ben was there to keep his younger brother from falling off his horse. He rode out of town in tandem with Will, keeping him upright. In his other hand he felt one of the money bags. He steered his horse with his knees.

Griff was having a good time. He was firing across the street at men who had taken cover behind horse troughs and barrels, but he didn't care. He felt alive.

"Griff!" Jake shouted, grabbing his brother's arm. "Let's go."

Ted was already riding out, and Jake pulled Griff to his horse with one hand while firing with the other. He'd already tied the second money bag to his saddle.

"Griff, damn it!"

"I'm coming, I'm coming," Griff said.

They mounted up and Griff said, "Damn, this was fun!" before a bullet struck him on the right hip, almost knocking him from his horse.

"Damn!" he said, in a totally different tone of voice.

TWELVE

"This is ridiculous," Clint said to Kate.

They were sitting together on a rock, and Clint's hands were tied in front of him.

"What do they hope to gain by keeping me here?" he asked.

"Belle told you what they want," Kate said. "Another night with you."

"I've never been in demand quite this way when it comes to sex," he said.

"I'm sorry, Clint," she said, "I really am. Maybe if I hadn't been insisting that you take me with you, you would have been gone by now."

"It's not your fault."

"Kate!" Belle called. "Stop talkin' to him and get over here."

"Here," Kate said, suddenly thrusting something at him. "Use it and get out of here."

As she walked away he tucked a knife between

his legs, waiting for the opportunity to use it to cut himself loose.

However, he had decided not to leave without Kate.
If they figured out that she had slipped him a knife, they
might kill her.

From everything he had heard about Ben Borton, if
he didn't get away from there before the Borton gang
returned, he would be just as dead.

His opportunity came later in the afternoon. The ladies'
chores took them to the nearby creek. Belle came over
and checked his bonds first, then tied his feet as well.

"What's that for?" he asked.

"Just to make sure you don't go nowhere while we're
at the creek. And if you do manage to wiggle or crawl
away, you'd probably die out there, all trussed up the
way you are."

"You're probably right."

She nodded and started away.

"Hey!"

She turned.

"When do we eat?"

"When we get back from the creek," she said.

He waited for her to follow Kate and Baby down to
the creek and then took out the knife Kate had left him
and started sawing at the ropes.

"Stop!" Ben called out to his brothers, and they all
reined in.

"Who's in one piece?"

"I am," Jake said.

"Ride back a ways and see if there's a posse comin' after us."

"Right, Ben."

"Ted, let's take a look at Will and Griff's wounds."

Ben and Ted dismounted, then helped Will and Griff off their horses.

"Ow, damnit, that hurts!" Griff complained.

As soon as Will's feet touched the ground, he keeled over. Ted managed to catch him before he hit the ground and lowered him gently onto his side.

"Will's hurt bad, Ben," he said, checking the wound in his younger brother's shoulder.

"I'm hurt, too," Griff grumbled.

"Pull your pants down," Ben said.

"What?"

"Pull down your pants so I can see the wound."

Still grumbling, Griff did as his brother asked.

"How is it?" he demanded.

"There's no bullet," Ben said, studying the wound. "It creased you, took out a nice chunk of meat, but the bullet's gone. We just got to stop the bleeding."

"Ben," Ted said, "I need help with Will."

"Right there."

"Hey," Griff complained, his pants around his ankles, "what about me?"

"Use your neckerchief to apply pressure," Ben said. "It'll stop soon."

"I could bleed to death!"

"Serve you right, I say, for standing straight up when bullets are flying."

Griff tried to stanch the bleeding with his neckerchief, bitching and moaning every moment.

Ben knelt by his younger brother and inspected the wound.

"It's bad," Ben said. "Will? You hear me?"

"Uh-huh," Will replied, weakly.

"You got to hold on, boy," Ben said. "You got to hold on until we can get you to Belle. She'll take proper care of you. You hear?"

"I . . . hear ya . . . Ben."

Ben looked at Ted.

"We got to get him back on his horse."

"Bouncing him around on a horse is likely to kill him, Ben," Ted said.

"We passed a small farm a ways back," Ben remembered. "We can go there. They're bound to have a buckboard."

"What about a posse?" Ted asked.

"Jake will come back and tell us if there is one. If there's not, then him and me will go and get that buckboard. We'll take Will the rest of the way in that."

"And me," Griff complained. "I can't ride, neither."

Ben looked at him and said, "If we get a buckboard, you can ride in it, too."

"Damn right," Griff said. "And I'll even hold the money bags."

Ted stood up, looked at his two bleeding brothers.

"I hope we got enough to make this worth it, Ben," he said.

"Yeah," Ben said, "me too."

THIRTEEN

They were all crouched by the creek, apparently doing laundry. Their guns were on the ground behind them, including Clint's gunbelt, which Belle had taken with her. He sneaked up close, going as quietly as he could, and reclaimed his gun.

"All right, ladies," he said, strapping it on, "that'll do for the laundry."

All three women straightened up and turned around to face him. Belle looked at her gun, lying at her feet.

"That wouldn't be a good idea, Belle," Clint said.

"You wouldn't kill a woman," she said, "especially not one you were with last night."

"You're right," he said, "I wouldn't—but that doesn't mean I wouldn't put one in an arm or a leg. How'd you like to limp around on one knee for the rest of your life?"

Belle bit her lips angrily and looked down at the gun again.

"Belle, don't," Kate said.

It took a moment, but Belle took her eyes off the gun and the muscles in her body seemed to visibly relax.

"All right," she said to Clint, "now what?"

"Now you kick those guns into the water."

"That'll ruin 'em."

"Once I'm gone you can take them out, clean them, oil them, and they'll be as good as new. Right now, though, I think we'd all be safer if they were in the water."

Belle glared at him and then kicked the weapons into the water.

"Now let's go back to camp."

"How did you get loose?" she demanded as they walked back, single file.

"You better learn to tie better knots," Clint said, so as not to give Kate away.

"Those knots were tight," she claimed.

"Apparently," he said, "not tight enough."

Jake came back with the news that a posse was not immediately on their trail.

"I thought there would be," Ben said, "the way those townspeople tried to protect their bank."

"I guess it's easier to do that than to get on a horse," Jake said.

As promised, Ben and Jake rode to the small farm they had passed.

"There's the buckboard," Jake said. It was sticking half in and half out of the barn. "Should we buy it?"

"Are you kidding?" Ben said. "Just go and hitch up the horses. I'll take care of anyone in the house."

"You ain't gonna—"

"I don't plan to, Jake," Ben said, "but I just don't see where it matters much, at this point."

Jake rode over to the barn and, as he dismounted, a man came out of the farmhouse, carrying a rifle. A teenage girl ran out behind him, yelling, "Papa, don't!"

Ben turned to face the man, to talk to him, but the farmer didn't want to talk. He raised the rifle and took aim at Jake.

"Don't, old man!" Ben yelled, but he didn't have time to see if the man would listen. He drew his gun and fired. His bullet struck the man in the belly, causing him to fire his rifle into the air before he fell forward onto his face. The girl bent over him.

Ben rode over to the house and looked down at the dead man. The girl looked up at him. He noticed two things. One, she was beautiful, and two, she wasn't crying.

"I'm sorry," Ben said, "he didn't leave me much choice."

"Well, now you went and did it," she said, standing up. "You know what you got to do now?"

"No," he said, "what?"

She smiled and said, "You got to take me with you."

"You won't get away with this," Belle said.

"Sure I will," he said. "I tie better knots than you."

He was tying her hands and feet, having already done the same to Baby.

"Ben and the others, they'll hunt you down for this," Belle said.

"Only if you tell them we had sex, and then they might kill you first. Think about it."

"What am I supposed to say when they come back and find us tied up?"

"Tell them you were robbed. I don't think you'll have that problem, though. Between the two of you, you should be able to untie each other after I'm gone."

"Two of us?" Baby asked.

"That's right," Clint said. "I'm taking Kate with me." He looked at her. "Go and saddle your horse."

"But . . . you can't do that," Baby said. "She belongs here."

"Stop it, Baby," Belle said. "She wants to go with him."

"But . . . why?"

"You can explain it to her, Belle," Clint said, "after we leave."

FOURTEEN

They put some distance between themselves and the Borton Gang's camp before they stopped. All during the ride, however, Kate had been looking over her shoulder.

"Are you sorry you left?" he asked.

"No," she said, "why?"

"You keep looking back."

"Well, it's not because I'm afraid I'm missing somethin'," she said. "I'm just afraid they're gonna come and get us."

"Maybe they will," Clint said, "but not for a while. Relax."

She righted herself in her saddle and asked, "Where will we go?"

"There's a town called Tierney near here," he said. "We can go there."

"That's where *they* went," she argued.

"Good," he said, "then that'll be the last place they'll look for you."

She looked as if she were about to argue, but then she realized how logical that was.

"Okay, then," she said, "let's go."

When the Bortons rode back into their camp, Belle and Baby were still trussed up. Clint Adams had, indeed, been better with knots than Belle was.

Belle and Baby watched with trepidation as the brothers rode in, bringing with them a buckboard and a woman—or a girl, actually.

"What the hell—" Ben Borton said when he saw that they were tied up.

"I'm glad you're finally back, Ben," Belle said. "Untie us."

"What happened here?" he demanded, dismounting.

"Clint Adams."

"The Gunsmith?"

"That's right," she said. "He rode in, tied up me and Baby and left with Kate."

"He stole Kate?"

"She went with him willingly, the bitch!" Belle said. "Come on, Ben, untie me."

"Did he take anything else? Horses, supplies?"

"No, just Kate."

"You let him take Kate, you bitch?" Jake demanded. Secretly, he had a crush on Kate, but now it was coming to the forefront.

"She said Kate went willingly, Jake," Ben said. "Relax. We need Belle to fix up Will and Griff."

"What happened to them?" Belle asked.

"They got shot is what happened to them. Untie her, Jake." Jake did so, but not before yanking on the ropes painfully, making her cry out. He was gentler with Baby, and soon both women were free.

"Come on, Baby," Belle said. "You got to help me. Bring some hot water."

She instructed the brothers to take both men out of the buckboard and lay them on the ground, where she could get at them. Belle had dug more lead out of these brothers and sewed them up than she could count.

She examined both men and decided that Will had to be worked on first.

"I'm bleeding here!" Griff shouted in complaint.

"You've stopped bleeding," she said, "but if you act up you're gonna start again. So be still!"

Griff grumbled, but obeyed.

"How's Will?" Ben asked.

"It's bad," she said, "but I've seen worse, and so have you. I think the bullet is lodged in a muscle. That saved him, because it kept it from his heart."

"Can you get it out?" Ben asked.

"Don't I always?"

"Yeah, Belle, you do," Ben said. "That's why I'm gonna let you finish what you're doin' before I make you tell me exactly what happened here."

"I'll tell you, Ben," she said. "I ain't never lied to you."

To herself she added, "Yet."

FIFTEEN

It took Sheriff Quentin Milo a few hours to assemble a posse. Most of the townsmen didn't mind firing at some men who were coming out of the bank, but when it came to getting on a horse and hunting the men down, most of them drew the line. In the end, Milo had only a half a dozen men, but with two of the Bortons injured, that might just be enough.

Clint and Kate rode into the posse on their way into town. Clint decided to stop, afraid that they might decided to chase them, thinking they were with the gang.

And, of course, one of them had been until very recently.

"Just let me do the talking," Clint said, as the seven riders approached.

"Why not just tell them where the camp is?"

"Look at them," Clint said. "The gang would have them for lunch."

"Why not tell them they need more men?"

"If the sheriff could get more men they'd be with him now," Clint said. "Just settle back and look pretty—but don't talk."

"Fine." She said it without sarcasm, as if she was used to such orders.

The posse approached, and the sheriff held up his hand to halt them about five feet from where Clint and Kate were standing their horses.

The lawman took a few moments to look them over. Clint figured that if he'd been alone he would have caught more of an attitude from this sheriff, but the posse was not looking for a man and a woman riding together.

"You folks on your way to Tierney?" he finally asked them.

"That's right," Clint said.

"Well, we had some ruckus there earlier today."

"What kind of ruckus?"

"A bank robbery."

"Did they get away with much money?" Clint asked.

"Some."

"Anybody get hurt?"

"Two dead," the lawman said, "but we wounded two of them, so they won't get far. Have you seen five riders together?"

"No, sir, we sure haven't." He looked at Kate. "Have we, dear?"

She shook her head. Apparently, when she promised not to talk she kept her promise.

"Well, when you get to town, don't be too hard on us at first," the lawman said. "We're still sort of recovering from what happened."

"We'll keep that in mind, Sheriff."

"Plan on stayin' long?"

"Just a day or two."

"Well, don't know if I'll get back before you leave," the man said, "but my name is Milo, Sheriff Quentin Milo." He seemed to be in his thirties and wore his badge without a hint of self-consciousness, as if he'd been wearing it a long time.

"Unusual name," Clint said. "I'll remember it."

The man opened his mouth to respond, but one member of the posse said, "Can we get goin', Milo? I got a store to run, ya know."

Milo looked at Clint and said, "Posses."

"I know what you mean."

"All right," Milo shouted to his posse, "let's keep movin'." He looked at Kate and added, "Sorry to have detained you, ma'am."

"Not at all," she said.

They watched as the posse rode away and noticed that they were riding in the wrong direction.

"Not a tracker among them," Clint said. "They'll never catch up to the gang."

"I wonder how far it is to town?" she asked. "I'm starved."

"Yeah," Clint said, "I could use a little something to eat myself."

SIXTEEN

Belle walked over to the fire, where Ben was sitting alone, drinking coffee.

"How is he?"

"I got the bullet out and the bleeding's stopped," Belle said. "Now we just have to wait and see."

"And Griff?"

"Bitchin' and moanin', as usual, but he's fine," she said.

"All right," Ben said. "Suppose you sit here and tell me what happened while we were gone."

Belle told him a story she had concocted while tied up. How Clint Adams had ridden in on them, pretending friendship, and then how he had turned on them and tied them up—except for Kate.

"Why would he take Kate?" Ben asked.

"Kate's the prettiest, Ben," Belle said, "you know that."

55

Ben reached out and touched Belle's still-smooth cheek and stroked it gently.

"Prettiest don't mean best, Belle."

"Tha—" she started, but he swung a backhand that caught her high on the cheek and knocked her flat on her ass.

"W-what was that for?" she demanded.

"For letting anyone ride into camp," Ben said. "You know better than that, Belle. You had guns, you could have stopped him."

"The Gunsmith? He would have laughed at three women with guns."

"Nobody laughs at anybody with a gun," he told her. "Now, was that the truth or is there something else you want to tell me?"

"It's the truth, Ben," Belle said, still holding her cheek. It stung, and felt warm. "Kate went with him on her own."

"Now why would she do that?" he asked. "We gave her everything she wanted. She was everybody's favorite, she got plenty of attention."

"Maybe too much," Belle said.

"Whataya mean, too much?"

"I mean on nights when you'd all take her she'd cry herself to sleep."

"So what?" he asked. "We're entitled to take any of you as much as we want."

"I guess she figured she was entitled to leave."

"Well, she figured wrong."

Belle got to her feet.

"Are you gonna go after her?"

"I'm thinkin' about it."

"Without Will and Griff?"

"I don't know."

If he went after Clint and Kate, Belle was afraid Kate would tell a different story, and Ben might believe her.

"I'll start a pot of stew," she said.

"You do that."

Ben continued to sip his coffee and consider his options. They had to move, because there *would* be a posse sooner or later. They could use the buckboard to take Will and Griff along until they could ride.

He looked over by the buckboard where the farm girl was sitting on the ground next to Will. She seemed to take a liking to him as soon as she saw him, and she still didn't seem upset about watching her old man get shot down in front of her. She was pretty enough, but Ben wasn't sure she had anything inside of her.

"Who's the girl?" Belle asked, as she set a big pot over the fire.

"Farm girl," Ben said. "We had to shoot her pa to get the buckboard. Old fool didn't give me a choice."

"So you took her along 'cause she was a witness?" Belle asked.

"We took her along 'cause she insisted," Ben said. "She said we killed her pa, and we had to take her with us."

"Why didn't you just kill her and leave her?"

"She's pretty," he said, "young and trainable."

"You want her to replace Kate?"

"She can't replace Kate," Ben said. "Two of her couldn't. Maybe when she gets a little older and fills out a little more, but not now."

Belle looked over to where the girl was sitting, next

to Will. She was putting a blanket over the youngest of the Bortons.

"Seems to have taken a liking to Will."

Ben laughed.

"He's the least threatening of us," Ben said.

"You gonna break her in?" Belle asked.

Ben dropped the remnants of his coffee into the fire and said, "I ain't all that sure she ain't already been broke in—maybe by her daddy."

"Her own father?"

"That's all I can figure as a reason she ain't screamed or cried since we killed him."

"That's sick!"

"Ain't it, though?" Ben asked. "Belle, when can Griff ride."

"In an emergency? Now. The wound is high up on his hip, wouldn't keep him from sitting a horse, if he had to."

"And Will?"

"That's gonna take longer, Ben," she said. "A lot longer."

If they moved out, there was no way he would leave Will behind. But with the buckboard, they'd never out-run a posse, or find Clint Adams and Kate.

"What are we gonna do?" Belle asked.

"Right now," he said, "you just get that food ready."

SEVENTEEN

When Clint and Kate rode into town, they saw what the sheriff was talking about. People were milling about aimlessly, still in shock from the events of the morning.

"This is good," Clint said.

"What is?" Kate asked. "That some of these people were killed?"

"No," he said, "but they're so shocked that no one is seeing us. No one will be able to describe us."

They found the livery and left both horses to be cared for, then headed for the nearest hotel.

"One room?" the clerk asked.

"Two," Clint said.

"Two?"

"She's my sister."

"Ah!"

The clerk handed over two room keys and said, "Oh, my bellboy is out, uh, over by the bank, gawking. We had some excitement."

"Oh?"

"Bank robbery. Two men killed."

"Too bad. Where's the sheriff?"

"Took a posse out after them."

"Good," Clint said, "maybe he'll find them. We don't need any help getting to our rooms. We only have our saddlebags."

"Well, have a nice stay, sir, ma'am."

"Thank you," Kate said, and followed Clint up the stairs.

"Your sister?" Kate asked when they reached the door to her room.

"I didn't know what else to say."

"You could've said I was your wife and saved the cost of the second room."

"I didn't know how you'd take that."

"We slept together on the ground, Clint," she said. "Remember? I'd kind of like to try it again, but in a real bed."

"I'll keep that in mind," he said. "I figured that after riding with that gang for so long you might enjoy having your own room."

They opened the door and peered inside.

"I'm not even sure what to do," she said.

"Get some rest," he told her. "I'll be back later and we'll get something to eat."

"What if—they show up?"

"I still think this is the last place they'll look," he said.

"But if they do?"

"I'll handle it."

"Five of them?"

"According to the sheriff, two are wounded. That might keep them where they are for a couple of days—especially with that posse going the wrong way."

She looked into the room again.

"Go on," he said, "go inside. There's nothing in there that will bite you."

"Clean sheets," she said, looking at the bed, "and I'm filthy."

"Would you like me to arrange for a bath for you?"

"Oh, yes, would you?"

"Sure," he said. "I'll have the desk man send someone up to tell you when the tub is ready."

"Hot water," she said, "real hot water."

"Hot water," he said, and closed her door with her on the other side.

When Clint left her alone in the room, Kate looked around nervously. She walked to the bed and pushed on the mattress with her hands, then put one knee on it and tested it. It had been a long time since she'd slept in a real bed—but was that worth getting killed over?

She had no doubt that if the Bortons found her they'd kill her—Ben would, for sure. She might be able to talk one of the others out of it, but not Ben. He'd feel betrayed, and she was sure that Belle had already told him that she went willingly.

To Ben, that would be the ultimate betrayal.

She walked to the window and looked down at the street. People were still milling about. Clint was right. They wouldn't come back here, not so soon, anyway.

She turned and walked back to the bed. It seemed very

inviting at the moment, but she didn't want to put her grubby, dirty body on those sheets until after she had a bath.

And after a bath, maybe she'd be able to get Clint Adams to join her. She remembered the things he'd done to her last night, with his mouth and his hands. She was looking forward to spending a whole night in a real bed with him doing those things—and her doing some to him.

EIGHTEEN

Clint left the hotel and walked over to the bank. There were even more people milling about there. He looked around and spotted a man wearing a badge, a young man of about twenty-five. Sheriff Milo had left his deputy behind to watch over things.

"What's going on, Deputy?" he asked, approaching the younger man. "Is there a run on the bank?"

"Huh?" The young man did not comprehend the term Clint used, one he himself had learned in New York.

"Is everyone taking their money out?" he said, clarifying his question.

"Oh, no sir," the deputy said. "Somebody took care of that already. Some fellers robbed the bank this morning, and killed two people."

"Ah, I see. Any idea who they were?"

"Somebody said they might have been the Borton gang, sir," the deputy said. "We don't know for sure, though."

"That's too bad."

"Be a while before we get back to normal here," the deputy said. "A while."

"But it will happen," Clint said. "Life goes on."

Suddenly, the deputy—nearly as tall as Clint, but skinny—turned to face him.

"And what are you doing in town, sir?"

"Just passing through," Clint said.

"What's your interest in the bank robbery?"

"No interest."

"But you came over here and asked me about it."

"Just out of curiosity," Clint said. "I actually came over to ask you if you knew a place to get a good steak dinner."

"There's a restaurant on Second Street called Papa John's," the deputy said. "Try there."

"Much obliged, Deputy," Clint said, "and good luck catching your robbers."

"Thank you," the deputy said, and Clint noticed that he'd left off the "sir" this time.

He knocked on Kate's door and, when she opened it, he saw a new woman looking at him. Her red hair was clean and lustrous. Her face and hands were also clean and she smelled fresh. The only drawback to her condition was that she had to wear the same clothes.

"Excuse me," he said, "I must have the wrong room."

"It's me, silly," she said. "You've just never seen me clean before."

"It *is* you, Kate!" he said, feigning surprise. "Well, you look so good I'm going to take you out to eat."

"At last!" she said. "I'm starving."

"Well, let's go."

"First," he said, putting his arm out to take, "we're going to get you something new to wear."

As they walked down the hall she said, "There's something you should know, Clint."

"What's that?"

"When I left the Borton camp I didn't take any money with me."

"You know what?"

"What?"

He smiled and said, "I don't care."

They stopped at the general store and got her a new pair of trousers and a new shirt, and Clint insisted on buying her a skirt with a fringe on it. He also insisted that she buy new underwear. When they left she was wearing everything new except her shoes. The store wasn't able to help them there. They didn't have her size.

"I have big feet," she lamented, outside.

Clint had her skirt, wrapped in brownpaper, under his arm. Her old clothes had been discarded on the spot.

"No, you don't," Clint said, "the rest of the women in this town have small feet."

She smiled and said, "Now I feel better."

"Ready to eat?"

"More than ready."

"I had a place recommended to me," he said, taking her arm this time. "Let's see if it's any good."

Clint found Papa John's with no trouble. It was too late for lunch, but early for dinner, so they had no difficulty getting the table he wanted. He sat across from Kate with his back to the wall and put her package down on the floor, beneath the table.

The little restaurant was "cute" according to her, with about ten tables covered by red-and-white checkerboard tablecloths.

"I wonder if Papa John is a real person?" she asked.

"I think we're about to find out."

She turned her head and saw an older man with a big belly, huge forearms, and slate gray hair coming toward them.

"God," she whispered, "I sure hope he's friendly."

NINETEEN

Papa John *was* friendly, and he welcomed them with a smile and open arms.

"Who sent you to my place?" he asked.

"Uh, the deputy," Clint said. "I didn't get his name."

"That would be Carl, Carl Mason. He's a good boy. Now, what can Papa John get for you?"

"Do you have a specialty?" Clint asked.

"All of my dishes are my specialty," Papa John said. "I am the best cook in the world."

"Would steak be too simple a thing to ask of the greatest cook in the world?" Clint asked.

Papa John laughed and said, "You're making fun of me, but you'll see. I'll make you the best steak you ever had. And you, Miss?"

"I'll have a steak, too," Kate said.

"All right," he said, "two steaks coming up, with vegetables and rolls."

"And coffee," Clint said. "How's your coffee?"

"Best in the world," Papa John said, immodestly.

Clint hoped so. In fact, he hoped that the meal was superb, because he knew that Papa John would ask them how it was, and Clint didn't want to do anything to get this huge man mad at him.

Kate must have been thinking along the same lines, because she leaned forward as Papa John left and asked, "What do we do if we don't like it?"

"That's easy," Clint said. "We lie."

But there was no need to lie. Not only was his steak the best Clint had ever had, so was the coffee. The man even managed to give a unique flavor to his vegetables.

He brought them a second pot of coffee and said it was on the house.

"Thank you, Papa John," Clint said.

"So, how did you like my steak?"

"You're right," Clint said. "You are the best cook in the world."

Papa John looked at Kate, and she nodded and said. "Definitely."

Papa John laughed and patted them both on the back.

"That's good," he said. "You can come back anytime you want."

"Thank you," Kate said.

Papa John left them to finish their coffee, and they realized that they had been so caught up in the experience of Papa John's meal that they'd forgotten everything else.

"I'd never have had an experience like this if I stayed with the Bortons," Kate said. "Thank you."

"Kate, can I ask you why you were with them in the first place?"

"It happened several years ago. They came to the town I lived in—it doesn't matter where—and I thought they were dashing and exciting, and I wanted to get out of there so bad . . . and that was that."

"And they took you along, just like that?"

"Those brothers need to have women around," she said. "To cook and do laundry and provide . . . other services."

"Was Belle with them when you joined up?"

"Yep," Kate said. "Other women have come and gone, but Belle's been there the longest."

"So other women have left them?"

"Well, not exactly."

"What do you mean?"

"Well," she said, "we'd wake up in the morning and one of the girls would be gone."

"But if she didn't leave, then . . ."

"That's what I thought," Kate said. "They killed her. The first time it happened I asked Belle about it, but she told me not to ask any questions. She said I didn't want to get any of them mad, or she might wake up one morning and find me gone."

"And what about Baby?"

"She's only been with the gang about six months— and she still likes it. She likes the attention. She thinks they love her, and she wants desperately to be loved, to be part of a family."

"Well, they are a family," Clint said.

"Yes," she said, "but they'll never accept a woman into the family. It's just the five brothers. They just want women like Belle . . . and Baby. . . . and me—for a while—who don't belong to any one man, but to the whole group.''

''So what do you want to do now?'' Clint asked.

''I think I have to get as far away from them as I can,'' she said. ''I'm going to go east and not stop until I can see the ocean.''

''I think that's a good plan,'' Clint said. ''You'll have to tell me where you end up. I might know someone there who can help you.''

''That would be great,'' she said. ''Thank you.''

She reached out and touched his hand and he took hers in his.

''Before I go east, though,'' she said, almost shyly, ''we still have tonight.''

''Yes,'' he said, rubbing her hand, ''yes, we do.''

They left Papa John's and went right back to the hotel to start the night early.

TWENTY

Jake Borton sat next to his brother Ben and asked, "Have you decided what we're gonna do?"

Ben looked around the camp. Except for him and Jake, everyone else was asleep.

"I think we've got to go to Tierney," he said.

"What?" Jake looked amazed. "Back to where we robbed the bank?"

His brother nodded.

"Why?"

"Two reasons," Ben said. "One, it's the last place they'd look."

"But the people—"

"We'll be able to walk down the street there and the people won't notice us," Ben said. "Trust me. Nobody remembers anything after the bullets stop flying."

"So what's the second reason?"

"Kate."

"What about her?"

71

"We can't let her get away with leavin'," Ben said. "Nobody's ever left us before, Jake."

"What makes you think that Kate is in Tierney?"

"Because she's with Clint Adams," Ben said. "He's smart. He'll take her there, figuring it's the last place *we'll* look."

Jake shook his head and said, "We came from the same place, Ben. How come you came out so smart?"

Ben looked over at his injured brother Will and said, "Yeah, right, smart."

"What are we doin' here?" one of the possemen asked Sheriff Milo.

"We need a place to bed down."

"At the Olson farm?" the man asked. "The old man'll shoot us on sight."

"Then I'll arrest him," Milo said. "We're commandeering his farm for the night, that's all. In fact, we'll sleep in the barn."

"That old man don't want nobody within spittin' distance of his daughter."

"You mean he still don't now that she's been broken in by every boy in the county?" Milo asked.

"Still thinks she's his sweet and virginal little girl," the other man said. He should know. His own boy, Fred, had been with her and bragged about it to his father, Vic Tucker. Tucker's attitude was, if she was givin' it out, why not take it? After all, his boy was all of fourteen, almost a man. He'd been with a woman—a whore—when he was thirteen.

"She's got him fooled, then."

They rode up to the house, and in the waning light Milo saw the man lying in the dirt.

"Damn it," he said, and dismounted. The other members of the posse stayed in their saddles, looking around nervously.

"Is it him?" Tucker asked.

"It's him," Milo said, "shot square in the heart."

Milo stood up and addressed the posse.

"Spread out and see what you can find."

"What are we looking for, Sheriff?" one man asked.

"Anything," Milo said. "Some indication that they might have stayed here, or taken something with them."

"Like his daughter, Bridget?" Tucker asked.

Milo looked at him and said, "Shit." He looked back at the posse and said, "See if you can find his daughter, while you're at it."

Bridget Olson was lying down next to the injured Will Borton. She couldn't thank the Borton gang enough for getting her away from her father. Many was the time she'd wanted to kill the old man herself and get away from him. He used to beat her mercilessly any time he thought she was having impure thoughts. What would he have done if he knew about all the boys she'd slept with—and men. Like their neighbor, Vic Tucker. First she'd seduced his son, and then the father, and she'd done it right in their own barn. Miz Tucker could have come out and caught her with her son in the morning, or her husband in the afternoon. Yep, Bridget had a lot of boys and men, but she was tired of it. Now she wanted one man, and she'd taken one look at Will Borton and decided he was the one. He was the youngest, and the best looking.

Now all he had to do was live.

"What about the girl?" Jake asked, looking across at Bridget Olson.

"We'll break her in," Ben said.

"My guess is she's already broke in," Jake said. "Look at the way she's lookin' at Will. When he sees her, he's gonna go—"

"Will knows the rules of our family," Ben said, cutting Jake off. "All the women are shared."

"Maybe he knows it," Jake said, "but she sure don't."

"Well," Ben said, "she'll find out, won't she?"

TWENTY-ONE

"Buckboard's gone, Sheriff," one of the posse members said.

"See, we did hit some of them," Milo said. "They need the buckboard to haul their wounded."

"That's gonna slow 'em down," Vic Tucker said.

"Yeah, it is," Milo said.

"Shouldn't we get going?"

"It's almost dark," Milo said. "We'll bunk here and head out in the morning. We'll follow the trail the buckboard makes."

"Ain't none of us trackers, Sheriff," another posseman said.

"We can follow the tracks of a wagon," Milo said. He was a piss poor excuse for a lawman if he couldn't do that, he thought. "Just find yourselves places to sleep tonight."

"What about somethin' to eat?" someone asked.

"You've got hard tack, eat that."

"And coffee?"

"We're running a cold camp," Milo said. "No coffee. Now go on, turn in. I want to get an early start in the mornin'."

As the men drifted away, Tucker asked, "What about old man Olson?"

"You and me, Vic," Milo said. "We'll bury him."

Clint surprised himself that night with his ability to keep up with Kate. She wanted to have sex with her on top, her on the bottom, next to each other, with him behind her. She wanted to pleasure him with her hands and mouth and then be pleasured with his hands and mouth. She wanted to do all this and more, and by the time they were done, only half the night was gone.

"I need a rest," he said, out of breath.

She got to her knees next to him and said, "I've never felt so alive."

"I can tell."

"How much rest do you need?"

"Just lie here next to me for a few moments," he said. "Let's talk a bit."

She lay down next to him and snuggled up against him. They were both naked, and the feel of her smooth, warm skin was so enjoyable he knew he wouldn't have to rest long.

"I'm a little surprised about something, Kate," he said.

"What's that?"

"Well, you told me how all the brothers would have sex with you, sometimes all in the same night."

"That's right," she said.

"I would think that would leave you not liking sex," he said. "How have you managed to avoid that?"

"I didn't like sex," she said, "that's true. When you had sex with Belle, and then Baby, they insisted that I had to, also. I actually came to you hoping you'd turn me away, or that you'd be too tired."

"And what happened?"

"*You* did," she said. "You touched me, touched my body the way no man ever has. You showed me that sex with a man can be . . . wonderful, and beautiful. And that just made me boiling mad at the Borton brothers for ruining it for me for so long."

"Well," he said, "I'm flattered—"

"You don't have to be flattered," she said. "You're a man who knows how make a woman feel good. Lucky for you, I haven't forgotten how to make a man feel good, even though it's been a while since I did it."

"And you do it real well," he said, sincerely. "I appreciate it."

"Do you appreciate it enough," she said, sliding her hand down to his crotch, "to show me—oh! I see that you do!"

Clint woke in the morning with Kate nestled between his legs. She was peppering his thighs, and then his penis and testicles, with little kisses designed to wake him up gently. Once she had his full attention, though—and his full size—she began to lick him in earnest, up and down the length of his cock, before taking it deep in her mouth and sucking it until he was on the verge of exploding. Only then did she mount him and stuff him inside of her and ride him until she was flushed and spasming with her own pleasure.

"I'm sorry," she said, later. "I used you that last time for my own pleasure."

"Believe me," he said, "there was plenty of pleasure in it for me."

"Now I'm hungry," she said. "I wonder if Papa John makes breakfast?"

"Why don't we get dressed," he suggested, "and go find out?"

She readily agreed.

TWENTY-TWO

When the rest of the Borton brothers woke up that morning, Ben gathered them around him.

"Ted, I want you to ride out and see where that posse is."

"Maybe there ain't one, Ben."

"There's a posse, all right," Ben said. "Just find them and see where they are."

"Okay."

"Go now!"

"I'm going."

"Belle, you check on Griff and Will."

"Yes, Ben."

"Make sure that girl helps you."

"I will."

"And find out her name!" he called after her.

"Baby, you make breakfast."

"Yes, Ben."

That left Ben standing next to Jake, the brother he was the closest to.

"What do you want me to do, Ben?"

"Jake, I want you to go to Tierney."

"What?"

"We talked about this last night."

"I know we did, but—"

"I'm tellin' you nobody will recognize you. You got to trust me on this."

"What do you want me to do there?"

"Lay low, but find if Kate is there, like I figure."

"What if Kate's layin' low?"

"Then you'll find out if the Gunsmith is there. If he is, then she is."

"Then what?"

"Then come back here and get us. Maybe while you're gone we'll get a bead on that posse."

"Okay, Ben," Jake finally said, "I'll trust you. I'll go to Tierney. But at the first sign that somebody recognize me, I'm headin' out."

"Good," Ben said, "that's what I'd want you to do."

Jake started to turn away, and then turned back.

"What?" his brother asked.

"What if she's in Tierney, Ben?"

"If she's there," Ben said, "we'll go in and get her out."

"And if she's still with the Gunsmith."

Ben hesitated and then said, "Then he's one dead legend."

TWENTY-THREE

Sheriff Milo had had to wake each and every member of his posse, all of whom complained about it, and about not having any breakfast.

"This is earlier than I get up to open my store," complained one.

"We've got to get an early start so we can catch up to these bastards before they get into the next county," Milo said. He knew that if that happened, his posse would quit him and return home.

"They might be in the next county already," another man said.

"Not with two wounded men," Milo said. "They've got to hole up somewhere until they heal up. That's our edge here, gentlemen."

"So how do we find them?" a man asked.

"We follow the buckboard tracks," Vic Tucker said, "right, Sheriff?"

"Right, Vic."

And that's what they were doing now. Milo was worried, though. If they came to ground that was too hard to hold the tracks, he was going to be lost, because he was no tracker, just a lawman.

And that's just what happened.

Ted Borton looked down from his position on a small rise at the sheriff's posse, which seemed totally lost. Borton figured that they had probably been following the buckboard tracks, but right now the ground beneath their feet was dry and cracked and incapable of holding such tracks.

And so, they were lost.

He quit the rise, mounted his horse, and rode back to camp.

It was an hour after Jake Borton left camp that Ted Borton came back.

"What'd you find?" Ben asked.

Ted told about the posse and how lost they seemed to be.

"How many men?"

"About six, counting the sheriff."

Ben rubbed his jaw.

"They probably don't have a tracker," he said. "If they go far enough, though, they'll pick up the trail again."

"What do we do?" Ted asked.

"Go out and cover the tracks that lead here, Ted," Ben said. "If they don't have a tracker, they might not notice that the tracks have been wiped out."

"Okay."

As Ted left, Ben walked over to where Griff was lying on the ground.

"How you doin', Griff?"

"Hurts like hell," Griff said. "How am I supposed to be doing?"

"Think you can ride?"

"Hell, no."

"Think you could ride if I told you you had to, or be left behind?"

"Hell, yes."

"That's what I thought."

"But I'll probably bleed to death in the saddle."

"That's a chance I'm willing to take."

"Thanks," Griff said. "What about Will? How is he doin'?"

"I was just going to ask Belle the same question," Ted said.

"Well, let me know."

"Will do."

Ben walked over to where Belle and the new girl, Bridget, were ministering to Will, whose eyes were open and clear.

"How you doin', Will?"

"I'll b-be okay, Ben," Will said, with youthful bravado. "I'll be read to go—you wait and see if I'm not."

"You won't be ready to ride for a while," Bridget said.

"Belle?" Ben asked.

"We can take him in the buckboard," she said, "but he can't sit on a horse. He'd fall out of the saddle."

"I would not."

"You would, too," Bridget said.

Will looked at her and said, "Who are you, anyway?"

"It doesn't matter who I am," she said. "I'm here, and I'm going to take care of you."

"Belle . . ." Ben said, again, this time jerking his head for her to accompany him.

"What?" she asked, when they were out of earshot of the girl and Will.

"Let her take care of him," Ben said.

"Why?"

"Because I said so."

"Fine."

"You've done enough," he said, "you dug out the bullet and sewed him up. She can do the rest."

"So what do I do?"

"Get this place ready to move," he said. "We'll be breaking camp sometime today."

"When?"

"That depends on what Jake says when he comes back from town."

"You still intend to go toward town?" she asked.

"Into town, if I have to," he said.

"We'll be noticeable, you know. The women, the buckboard—"

"You let me worry about that, Belle," he said. "Just get ready to strike camp, and have Baby help you."

"Okay, Ben."

Ben found himself an empty corner, took his gun from his holster, and started to clean it. Sometime later, Ted returned and reported that he had wiped out the buckboard tracks for miles.

"Good," Ben said. "It will take them a while to find

it again—or maybe they'll just turn and go the wrong way altogether."

"Do you think?"

"You saw them," Ben said. "How did they look?"

"Like a bunch of store owners on horseback," Ted said. "Ben, I think we could take them."

"I'm not getting into any shorthanded gun battles, Ted," Ben said. "If Griff could shoot, maybe, but not without Griff *and* Will."

"Okay," Ted said, "you're the boss."

"I'm not the boss," Ben said, "I'm the head of the family."

"Right," Ted said, "the head of the family."

"Belle's gettin' ready to strike the camp. Take a look at all the horses and see if they're ready to go, okay?"

"Okay, Ben."

Ben sat on a rock and put his gun back together. Nobody had ever challenged his authority as the older brother, but lately he'd started to see possibilities in Griff. He was impatient with some of the decisions Ben had made. Ben hoped he would not have to prove his superiority to his brothers. He hated the thought of hurting one of them.

But as long as they did what they were told, that would never happen.

TWENTY-FOUR

Papa John did, indeed, serve breakfast, and it was every bit as good as the dinner had been the night before. Over breakfast they decided that the best course of action for Kate was to get on a stagecoach east and just keep on going.

"I don't have the mon—" she began, but he cut her off.

"I'll buy you a ticket."

"You're going to have to let me know where I can send all this money you've spent on me," she said, "when I get on my feet."

"Don't worry about it." he said. "It's worth it to get you away from the Bortons."

"And what are you going to do?" she asked.

"I'll leave town right after you do," he said. "That way we'll both be gone before anyone—the Bortons or the law—get back."

They walked over to the stage line to find out when

the next stagecoach was leaving. As it happened, it was in one hour.

"You can make that," Clint said to her. "You don't have much to pack."

"Or anything to pack in."

"We'll get you a carpetbag."

He bought her a ticket.

"How fur do ya want ta go?" the clerk asked.

"As far as she can get on one ticket."

The man handed Clint the ticket, he paid for it, and then turned and handed it to Kate.

"You're all set. Now all we have to do is get you packed and check out of the hotel."

As they walked back to the hotel she asked, "Which way will you be heading?"

"North," he said. "I've got a friend I'd like to see in Denver."

"You sure you wouldn't want to ride east?"

"Got to go north, Kate. It's better that way."

"I know," she said. "I just thought I'd ask."

Clint checked out while Kate packed her things and met him in the lobby. They left together and walked over to the depot. Two other people—a drummer, and an older man—were also waiting for the stage.

"You don't have to wait, Clint," Kate said. "I can get on myself."

"I'll feel better if I put you on and watch it pull out."

"I wish . . ." she said.

"You wish what?"

"Oh, I just wish we had a little bit more time together."

"The time we spent together was great, Kate."

"Wasn't it?"

"It was."

They sat together and talked, and when the time came closer for her to leave she reached out for his hand and he let her hold it, squeezing her hand back a little.

"Okay, folks," the driver came in and called out, "we're ready to leave."

The passengers stood up, and Clint walked Kate out to the stage. The older man was about to climb in when Clint said, "Excuse me," and pushed past him.

"Hey!" the man said.

"Ladies first," Clint replied, and helped Kate into the coach.

"Now you can get on," Clint said to the man.

The man made a sound like "harumph," gave Clint a dirty look, and got on.

"No manners," the drummer said to Clint. "Don't worry, Mister, I'll make sure he treats your wife with respect."

Clint didn't bother to correct the man and simply said, "Thanks."

The last he saw of Kate she was leaning out the window, waving vigorously.

Clint went from the depot to the livery, saddled Duke, and rode out of Tierney, thinking that he had left all that trouble behind.

Little did he know . . .

TWENTY-FIVE

Jake Borton marveled at his brother's ability to be right. He rode into town and no one raised a fuss; no one pointed at him or yelled "bank robber" or "killer." He rode to the nearest saloon, which wasn't open yet, but left his horse tied to a post in front of it. Then he started walking around. It wasn't until he saw Kate on the street, walking with a man, that he took refuge in a doorway so she wouldn't see him.

He saw that she was carrying one piece of luggage and followed them to the stage line depot. Apparently, one or both of them were getting on a departing stage. When they went inside the depot, he crossed the street and started looking for the coach. He found it in an alley, on the side of the building. A man was cleaning out the inside, and when he walked away to discard the trash, Jake went into action. He approached the coach, decided on a rear wheel, and loosened the lynch pin that held the wheel to the axle. He figured that after a few miles of travel, the vibrations would cause the pin to fall out and the wheel to come off. With any luck, it would break. That would give him and his brothers time to catch up to it.

He got away from the coach before anyone could see him, reclaimed his horse from in front of the livery, and rode back to camp.

"One or both?" Ben asked. "It's a simple question."

"I didn't wait and see, Ben," Jake said. "What does it matter if she's on the coach alone, or with him?"

"It matters a helluva lot if we don't want to get killed."

Jake frowned and said, "I'm sorry, I just didn't think—"

"Well, think now. Was she carrying a bag?"

"Yes."

"And was he?"

"No."

"Saddlebags?"

Jake frowned, trying to remember.

"No."

"Okay, then, chances are he's just putting her on the stage and then going his own way."

"That's good."

"That's very good. What did you do about the coach?"

"In a little while they should be losing a wheel."

"That's good," Ben said. "You and I can do this, Jake. The others can stay here."

"Fine by me. Will would slow us down, anyway."

"Come on, we'll tell the others . . ."

• • •

When the wheel came off, the coach listed to one side, and the wheel kept going.

"Tarnation!" Pete Vincent, the driver yelled, as he saw the wheel go by him. "Whoa, team!"

He pulled the team to a half before more damage could be done.

"Got another wheel?" asked Mel Jennings, who was riding shotgun.

"No, damnit," Pete said. "We'll have to go and get it and hope it's in one piece. I better tell the passengers."

Both he and Jennings stepped down in time to be yelled at by the older man, David Reed.

"What's the meaning of this?" he demanded. "Why have we stopped?"

"You see the way this coach is leaning to one side?" Vincent asked.

"So?"

"That means we lost a wheel."

"So put another on."

"We don't have another one."

"Well then, what—"

"You mind if I let the other passengers in on this?" he asked. He looked past Reed, who by now was standing outside. The other people, Kate and the drummer, whose name was Sam Webb, were each looking out a window.

"Folks, seems like we lost a wheel. Jennings and I are gonna go and chase it down. If it's in one piece, we'll be able to put it back on, somehow."

"And if it's not?" Webb asked.

"Well, why don't we face that if we come to it?"

Vincent said. "I suggest you folks step down and stretch your legs. It might be a while."

"This is the most ridiculous thing I ever heard . . ." Reed was saying, but both Vincent and Mel Jennings walked away, tuning the man out.

Who knew how far that wheel could have rolled before it came to a stop?

Ben and Jake Borton skirted the town, making better time by avoiding it, and picked up the trail of the stagecoach. It took only a few miles, but they finally came upon it, stopped and listing to one side.

"Well, well, Jake," Ben said, "looks like it happened just the way you said it would."

"Yeah, Ben."

"Let's go."

TWENTY-SIX

Sheriff Milo got lucky. He'd ridden ahead of the rest of the posse to scout about and see if he could pick up the buckboard trail again. He was no tracker, but he wasn't totally inept, either. He knew when a trail had been brushed out. He found it, kept going, and eventually found the trail again. Whoever had tried to brush it out was more inept than he was.

Somebody had underestimated him and was going to pay for it.

He turned and rode back to the rest of the posse.

Ted Borton was sitting at the fire having a cup of coffee when the posse came riding in. Belle and Baby were packing things away, while Bridget was still sitting by Will's side. Griff was lying under the buckboard, out of sight, trying to get some sleep.

When the posse came in there were six of them, led by a lawman. Ted saw them first and drew his gun. He fired first, even though they all had rifles or shotguns in their hands. They were storekeepers by trade and were reluctant to pull the trigger at first. It cost one of them his life.

The bullet took one of the posse off his horse and alerted the rest of the camp.

Sheriff Milo snapped off a shot at Ted, missing, and then felt a bullet whiz by him that came from somewhere else. He couldn't see that Griff Borton was firing on them from beneath the buckboard.

Lead was flying all around now, and since the posse was bunched, they were getting hit hard.

"Spread out, spread out!" Milo shouted.

Belle grabbed her gun and started firing as well. Baby, however, as she turned with her gun to fire, was hit twice, once in the hip, which spun her around, and then in the back, a shot that killed her instantly.

Milo's command to spread out had come too late. Between Ted, Belle, and Griff—none of whom had any qualms about firing their guns—the posse was decimated. Four were dead, and one was hanging from his saddle. When a bullet struck the sheriff in the shoulder, he knew they had to get out of there before they were all killed. He and the remaining member of the posse who was also wounded, rode out of camp even faster than they had ridden in.

Now, who had underestimated whom?

"Well," David Reed said, "maybe we'll have some help, after all."

"Whataya mean?" the drummer, Webb, asked.

"Two riders coming," Reed said.

Kate had been nervous ever since the wheel came off. Now she looked into the distance at the two riders and recognized Ben Borton's sorrel. It had to be Jake next to him.

"Oh, God," she said. "That's not help."

"What?" Webb asked.

"What are you talking about, young lady?" Reed said. "Of course they'll help."

"Do either of you have a gun?"

"Why would I need a gun?" Reed asked. "I'm a banker."

"I don't have one, either, Miss," Webb said.

"Then we better find the driver and the other man, and fast," she said. "We've got trouble."

She started away, but neither man moved to follow her.

"If you stay here you'll be killed," she said. "I know those men."

"Are they after you?" Reed asked. "Is that why you know them?"

She hesitated, and then said, "Yes."

"Then I'll stay," the banker said. "They won't harm me."

"You're being foolish."

"I don't appreciate being called a fool, young lady. We shall see who the fool is."

"Mr. Webb?" she said.

Webb thought a moment, and then said, "All right, I'll come with you."

He and Kate left David Reed standing by the coach, awaiting the arrival of Ben and Jake Borton.

TWENTY-SEVEN

Clint put twenty miles between himself and Tierney before he decided to stop for supplies. He hadn't bought any in Tierney because he just wanted to get away from there.

He stopped in a small town called Bakersfield, which had one hotel, a general store, one saloon, and, surprisingly enough, a telegraph office. He reined Duke in right in front of the general store and went inside. Several moments later he came out with a canvas sack that contained coffee, some fried meat, and several cans of fruit. This would hold him for a while.

He mounted Duke and intended to ride out of town immediately, but they had to go right past the saloon, and suddenly he developed a powerful thirst that he just knew would not be satisfied by a few sips of water from his canteen.

He reined Duke in again and went inside for a beer.

• • •

David Reed stood quite still as the two riders approached. When they reached him, he put up a hand and waved.

"Nice of you fellas to stop," he said. "We're having some trouble here."

"Where's the woman?" Ben Borton asked.

"What woman?"

Ben drew his gun and shot the banker in the right knee. Reed fell to the ground, shrieking.

"I'll ask again," Ben said. "If I don't get the answer I want, I'll shatter the other knee. After that I'll move on to your elbows."

"No, no, no," Reed screamed, waving a bloodstained hand at Ben. "She went that way, looking for the driver and the shotgun."

"How many men with her?"

"Two . . . no, three. There's a drummer, but he's not armed."

"See?" Ben asked. "Was that so hard?"

"Please," Reed said, blubbering now, "please, I need a doctor . . ."

"No," Ben said, "you don't," and shot the man in the heart.

When Kate and the drummer, Webb, found the driver and the shotgun, they were both bent over the wagon wheel, which had come to a stop in a gulley, shaking their heads. They looked up as the other two approached.

"It's busted," the driver said.

"Can't be fixed," the other man said.

"We have worse news," Kate said, and told them about the two men.

"Maybe Mr. Reed is right," the driver, Vincent, suggested. "Maybe they just want to help."

"Maybe she's right, Pete," Mel Jennings said. "She says she recognized them. What do we do if they come after us?"

"You've got a shotgun, don't you?" Webb asked.

"They're not after us," Jennings said. "They're after her!"

"Are you saying you won't help me?" Kate demanded.

"Lady," he said, "I signed on to ride shotgun, not to get myself killed for your personal business."

"Well . . . give me the shotgun, then," she said. "I'll protect myself."

"Give *me* the shotgun," the drummer said. "I'll protect her."

"I ain't givin' neither of you my shotgun," Jennings said. "It's mine, I had to pay for it myself."

Kate looked at Vincent.

"Do you have a gun, Mr. Vincent?"

"I've got a rifle."

"Good."

"It's under the seat of the coach."

"Damn," Webb said.

At that moment, they all heard the first shot.

"See?" Kate said. "Mr. Reed is finding out now that I was right."

"Maybe they're just trying to scare him," Jennings said.

At the sound of the second shot, they all jumped.

"That's it," Jennings said, "I'm getting out of here."

"Coward," Webb said.

"A live one," Jennings said. "You comin', Pete?"

"The coach is my responsibility, Mel," Vincent said. "I can't go."

"Well then, good luck," Jennings said, and started walking away.

"Wait!" Kate yelled. "If anything happens, you be sure to tell people it was the Borton brothers!"

"I'll tell 'em!"

"You got to forgive Mel," Vincent said. "He ain't a brave man."

"What's he doing riding shotgun for the stagecoach then?" Webb asked.

"Seems like an easy job when you ain't carrying a payroll or somethin'."

"Well," Webb said, "what do we do now?"

"Reed is bound to have told them which way we went," Kate said. "I thank you gentlemen for staying with me, but there's no need for you to die, too. We should just split up."

"Can't do that, Ma'am," Webb said. "I promised your husband I'd look out for you."

"Husband?"

"That feller who put you on the stage."

"Oh, that wasn't my husband, just a friend. Clint Adams."

"The Gunsmith?" Vincent asked. "Man, if he was riding with us now we'd have no trouble."

"But he's not, Mr. Vincent," Kate said. "Again, I say we split up."

"They'll track you easy, Miss," Vincent said. "You ain't got big feet like we do."

"What do we do, then?" Webb asked.

"We'll have to circle around and try to get to the stage for my rifle," Vincent said. "You go one way, I'll go the other, one of us is bound to get to it. It'll even the odds up, some." He looked at Kate. "Miss, you might as well wait here, out of sight. Don't wander off, or they'll find you for sure." Then he looked at Webb again. "Let's go, Mr. Webb."

"Good luck," Kate said, but she knew in her heart they'd need more than luck against the Borton Boys.

She also knew in her heart that she was as good as dead.

TWENTY-EIGHT

Kate did as the driver of the coach suggested and stayed where she was. She sat and listened for the sound of more shots, but none came. That was odd. If Webb and Vincent were caught trying to get to the rifle under the seat, there would have been shots. If they had actually gotten the rifle, there should have been some shots. The fact that it was quiet made her nervous. She knew that Ben Borton was almost as lethal with a knife as he was with a gun. She decided to now disregard Vincent's advice and try to find out what was going on.

She left the gulley and circled the way she had seen the driver do. Before long she came within view of the crippled coach. There was no sign of anyone near it, though. She looked around, but saw no one. She started to walk to the coach, still wary in case someone came into view. Nothing happened until she had almost reached the coach, and then the door opened and two bodies tumbled out. Vincent and Webb, both with their throats cut from ear to ear.

She stopped short.

Behind the bodies came Ben and Jake Borton, and Ben was smiling.

That was always a bad sign.

Mel Jennings, after he left Kate, Webb, and Vincent, managed to flag a ride from a buckboard that was going back to Tierney. He knew the people, a family who had a farm nearby, and so he felt safe riding with them.

"What's goin' on?" the farmer asked.

"Stagecoach was hit," Jennings said. "I got to get to the sheriff."

"Well, hop on."

He did.

"Hello, Kate," Ben said.

Kate said nothing.

"I see you got yourselves a couple of heroes here," he said, looking down at the dead men. "What happened to the Gunsmith? He leave you when he found out how worthless you are?"

"We split up," she said. "I went my way, and he went his."

"Well," Ben said, "then I guess it's time for you to come back home, huh?"

"I ain't."

"What?"

"I said I ain't goin' with you, Ben. I can't take it with you Bortons anymore."

Ben spread his hands.

"Are we that bad, Kate?"

"Yes," she said, "you're worse than bad."

"Now that hurts, Kate, that really does. I thought we was family."

"You and your brothers," she said, "that's all the family you know and want. You're all sick!"

"So I take it that means you don't want to come back to us? Back to your friends?"

"I have no friends there."

"You're ungrateful, Kate," Jake said, "that's what you are."

"Shut up, Jake," she said. "Ben didn't give you permission to talk."

"I don't need Ben's—"

"Shut up, Jake," Ben said.

"See?" she said to Jake. "Nobody's allowed to talk unless Ben says so."

"Don't listen to her, Jake," Ben said. "She's just trying to stir up trouble."

Ben came closer to Kate, so close she could feel his breath on her, but she didn't move. If she was going to die she was going to do it standing up to him.

"I'll give you one more chance to come back Kate, but you have to say please this time."

"I'd rather die."

"I thought you might say that."

She didn't realize that he was still holding his knife until he thrust it into her belly.

"It's a shame, Kate," he said, "a damn shame. You were always the prettiest."

Those were the last words she ever heard.

TWENTY-NINE

As soon as Mel Jennings got back to town, he went to the sheriff's office. He had no way of knowing that the sheriff and what was left of his posse—one man—had returned while he was gone. He walked in and saw the deputy behind the desk.

"Deputy," Jennings said, "we got trouble with the stage."

"What's your connection?" Carl Mason asked.

"I was riding shotgun when we got hit by the Borton Boys."

"The Bortons?" the deputy got to his feet. "Where are the others? The driver and the passengers?"

"They stayed behind."

"You've got the shotgun," the deputy said. "Why didn't you stay and fight?"

"Well, somebody had to come for help."

"You could have left the shotgun behind for them."

Jennings cradled the shotgun and said, "It's mine. I paid for it with my own money."

"I hope it was worth every cent to you," Deputy Mason said. "Come on."

"Where?"

"You're gonna take me to the stage."

"Where's the sheriff?"

"He came in all shot up by the Borton Boys," the deputy said.

"Jesus!"

"Don't worry," the deputy said. "He was west of town, and you were east. If you both got hit by the Bortons, it means they split up."

"That's what the girl said," Jennings replied. "That there were two of them."

"Which girl?"

"The one Clint Adams put on the stage."

"Adams?" The deputy frowned. "He was in town?"

"He was," Jennings said. "But ain't no more."

"All right," the deputy said, "we can talk more later. Let's get you a horse and you can show me where you were hit."

"W-what if they're still out there."

"Well," Mason said, "if there's only two of them, between you with your shotgun and me, we'll be even, won't we?"

"We will?" Jennings asked, shrilly.

"Come on."

The deputy sat his horse and surveyed the grim scene. The passengers were dead, as was the driver. He dismounted to check each body, even though he knew what he would find. They were all dead. One was shot, the other two men had their throats cut, and the woman had been gutted. It might even have taken her a while to die.

"This was cruel," he said.

"Can we get out of here?" Jennings asked. He and his horse were skittish.

In reply, Carl Mason walked over to him, dragged him off his horse, and pulled him over to where the woman was lying, still clutching her belly in death, as if in labor with a child.

"See that?" he asked. "This might have been avoided if you'd left them your shotgun. If you hadn't run out on them."

Jennings pulled away and then backed away from the deputy, one hand held out in front of him.

"What would be the point of me stayin' and dyin', too?" the man demanded.

"The point is maybe nobody would have died."

"Come on, Deputy," Jennings said. "These are the Bortons we're talkin' about. Did they try to kill the sheriff? He couldn't stop them, so what makes you think one shotgun could have?"

The deputy looked down at the once vibrant, beautiful woman and said, "You could have tried, man. You could have tried."

THIRTY

The only reason Clint was still in Bakersfield to hear the news was because he'd managed to find himself a fairly decent poker game which, in a town this small, was a surprise.

He'd been playing for hours when a man came running in with the news.

"The Tierney stage was hit by the Borton Boys," the man said.

"How bad?" somebody shouted.

"Bad," the man said. "All the passengers were killed, and the driver. The fella riding shotgun was the only one to get away."

When the man finished his pronouncement, he went to the bar for a beer.

"Cash me out," Clint said to the table.

"But . . . you got all the money," one of the men complained.

"That's because you're such a bad player, sir," Clint said. "Now cash me out."

The no-nonsense look on his face—and the fact that they knew who he was—kept the other four players from complaining too much.

Clint got up while they counted his money and went to the bar where the man with the news was.

"Was there a woman on that stage?" he asked.

"What?"

"Listen carefully," Clint said, grabbing the front of the man's shirt. "Was there a woman on it?"

"A woman?" the man said. "Yeah, yeah, I think they mentioned a woman."

"And the man riding shotgun got away?"

"That's right. He brought the news back to Tierney, went out with the deputy to bring back the bodies."

"Who did you hear all this from?"

"The news is spreading, friend," the man said. "I don't even remember who I heard it from."

"Then are you sure you heard it right?"

"Let him go, Mister," the bartender said. "He's just tellin' you what he heard."

Clint released the man and went back to the table to collect his money. He was going to have to ride back to Tierney tonight, in the dark, to find out for sure if Kate was alive or dead.

When Ben and Jake Borton got back to their camp, they were greeted enthusiastically by Ted.

"We got 'em," he said.

"Got who?" Ben asked.

"The posse. They rode right on in here, slick as you

please, a bunch of storekeepers with guns."

"And?"

"And we shot the hell out of them. Killed four of 'em, wounded the other two—including the sheriff."

"You did all that?"

"Me, Griff, and Belle—she was shootin', too."

"Well, well," Jake said, "either we don't have to worry about a posse anymore, or we have to start worrying about a bigger one."

"There's another worry we might have," Ben said.

"What's that?" Jake asked.

"Depending on how the Gunsmith felt about Kate," Ben said, "we might have him after us, too."

"He's just one man," Jake said, but it was plain that he didn't believe his own words.

"Don't worry," Ben said, to both brothers, "I can handle Clint Adams."

Neither brother was sure of that, but they nodded their heads anyway.

And then Ted told Ben about Baby.

THIRTY-ONE

Clint reached Tierney well after nightfall. He went to the nearest saloon and asked questions until he found out where the deputy lived. Then he went and pounded on the man's door until he answered.

"What the hell—oh, it's you," the deputy said, rubbing his face. He'd obviously been asleep, and just as obviously lived alone. "You were asking questions about the bank robbery."

"My name's Clint Adams, Deputy," Clint said. "I have to talk to you."

"Adams," the young man said, wide-eyed, and then he composed himself and said, "Come in."

He had two rooms and no kitchen. Slept in one, sat in the other.

"Have a seat."

"I'll stand."

"I know why you're here."

"Do you?"

"You heard about the stage."

"Then it's true?"

"It's true?"

"The woman? She's dead?"

"They were all dead," the deputy said. "One man had been shot in the knee and the heart. The driver and the drummer had their throats cut. The woman . . ."

"Yes?"

"She'd been stabbed in the belly and left to die."

"What's the sheriff going to do about it?" Clint demanded.

"Not much, the shape he's in," the deputy said. "He and the posse found some of the Borton Boys and got shot up for their trouble. Only two of 'em came back."

"Well, what are you going to do?"

"Me?"

"You're the law now, aren't you? Acting sheriff until he gets back?"

The young man scratched the top of his head and said, "I guess I am."

"Put together a posse."

"Mister Adams," he said, "after what happened to the first one ain't nobody gonna volunteer for the second, believe me."

"I will," Clint said. "I'll volunteer for the posse. It can be you and me, if it has to be."

Now the young man rubbed his jaw.

"It's your job," Clint said.

"Don't try to tell me my job," the young deputy said, showing sand. "It ain't my job to get myself killed goin' against impossible odds."

For once, the Gunsmith traded on his reputation.

"There aren't any impossible odds for me, Deputy. You should know that."

"I do, sir," he said, "I do, and I'll go with you, but not because it's my job. I don't like what they did to that lady."

"Then you won't be going with me, *Sheriff*," Clint said, putting out his hand, "I'll be going with you."

THIRTY-TWO

Clint got himself a hotel room, but he didn't sleep much that night. He kept berating himself, and blaming himself, for Kate's death. He'd talked to the deputy about paying for her burial, but it turned out that had been taken care of. She'd already been buried. He decided that before he left town, he would buy her a proper headstone. If he'd just stayed with her instead of riding off on his own . . . But how was he to know the Bortons would find her? How had they known she was on that stage? Clearly, they must have had someone in town who saw her board, someone who took the news back to them—maybe even one of them.

What gall, he thought, to send one of them back into a town where they had robbed the bank and killed people. It took gall, and luck, and, apparently, it had worked.

Five men, five brothers, Clint figured. There was no way he could assume that some of them had been injured during the robbery. Better to expect five men with guns in their hands. He'd faced those kinds of odds before, but he usually had somebody like Bat Masterson or Wyatt Earp backing his play—or he, theirs. Here he had an untried deputy watching his back.

That was a good way to get killed.

"You want to what?" Jake Borton asked Ben.

"Go back," Ben said.

"For Chrissake, why?"

"Because we never got into the safe," Ben said. "Do you know how much we got the first time?"

"About five thousand," Jake said. "I thought that was a good haul."

"Five thousand from the tellers' cages," Ben said. "How much do you think is in that safe, then?"

"I don't know," Jake said. "A lot."

"Right," Ben said, "and would they expect us to come back?"

"Hell, no," Jake said. "I don't even expect us to go back."

"Exactly," Ben said.

"That's not the only reason you want to go, is it?" Belle asked.

She, Ted, and Griff had been listening to the conversation, not contributing anything until now.

"Whattaya mean?" Ben asked.

"You want to get that town back because they made you run," Belle said. "They made you leave before you could get into the safe."

"So, what if I do?" Ben asked. "Look, I think we ought to hit that bank and then set fire to it. The locals will be so busy fighting the fire they won't even think of us."

"That whole side of the street might catch fire," Ted pointed out. "The buildings are real close together."

"So what?" Ben asked, again. "Who's with me?"

"I am," Griff said. "I owe those people something."

"Can you ride, Griff?" Ben asked.

"I'll ride."

"Ted?"

"I'm in, Ben."

"Jake?"

"Sure," Jake said, "why not? Let's make it a family affair."

"I want to come," Belle said.

"You can't," Ben said. "Somebody has to stay here with Will."

"Who's gonna hold the horses?" she asked. "Ted can't stand watch and hold the horses."

"She's right, Ben," Ted said.

"What about Will?" Ben asked.

"He'll be all right until we come back," Belle said. "Hell, he sleeps most of the time and Bridget can look after him."

Ben was thinking that it was too bad the posse had killed Baby, or they wouldn't have this problem.

"All right, then, Belle," Ben said. "You can come along."

"Yes!"

"But you have to do exactly what I say."

"I will," she said. "Don't I always?"

"No," he said, "but this time if you don't, it could get us killed, so I need you to swear."

"I swear, Ben," she said. "I swear."

"Okay, then," Ben said, rubbing his hands together, "we're going back."

THIRTY-THREE

Carl Mason was worried. He was about to go after the five Borton brothers, just he and Clint Adams. Now, he knew all about Adams's Gunsmith legend, and the man had stayed alive for a lot of years depending on his gun, but what about him? When the lead started flying, Adams was going to be looking out for himself, not for Carl Mason.

This had to be done, of course, or else he'd have to turn in his badge. With the sheriff down, the deputy had to step up and do the job. All his life all he'd wanted to be was a lawman, and then Quint Milo gave him the chance. If he didn't do this, he'd be letting the town, Milo, and himself down.

Still, he decided to go and talk it over with the sheriff. When he knocked on the door, his heart started pounding, because he knew who was going to answer it.

"Carl," Mary Milo said when she saw him. Mary was ten years older than Carl Mason, but that hadn't stopped the two of them from having an affair behind the sheriff's back. This was something Mason was not proud of. It happened last year, when he was twenty-four and new to the job. Mary saw him with her husband one day and, she told him, set her cap on him. It didn't take her long to seduce him with her long hair and her smooth, fragrant skin. He had never been with a woman other than a whore up until that time. He loved the way her small, tea-cup breasts felt in his hands, and how her ass felt when she was sitting on top of him, with his penis buried away up inside of her. She bemoaned the fact that she and Milo didn't have sex anymore. He was just too tired all the time, and Mason wondered how any man married to a woman like Mary Milo could be too tired to have sex with her.

But the guilt finally won out, and he called it off just a few months ago. He did everything he could to avoid her since then, but there was no way to do it now.

"Hello, Mary."

She touched her hair and said, "I haven't seen you in a while."

"I've been . . . busy."

"I'm sure," she said, tossing her long hair back over her shoulder. The movement brought his eyes to the hollow of her throat, and he remembered the time he had spent smelling that place, and kissing it.

"I came to see the sheriff."

"I figured," she said. "I didn't think you'd come to see me."

"Is he awake?"

"Sure," she said. "Come on in."

They went to the living room and she said, "I was

just going to get him some coffee. Go upstairs and I'll bring some for both of you.''

''Thanks.''

He watched her walk to the kitchen and then shook his head to dispel the thoughts he was having and went up to the bedroom she shared with Sheriff Milo.

''Hey, Carl,'' Milo said as he entered the room. ''Good to see you, boy.''

Mason knew that he would not have been so glad to see him if he'd know what Mason had been up to with his wife.

''Hi, Sheriff.''

''What brings you here?''

''Got a problem.''

''You do? Well, sit down and we'll hash it out.''

Milo had been hit in both shoulders. He hadn't found this out until he got back to town and saw the doc. He couldn't move either arm very well and had to be fed his meals. For that reason, he didn't enjoy eating, because it made him feel helpless. Add to that the fact that he and his wife had not been getting along for longer than he cared to remember, and it made eating an unpleasant experience for both of them.

Mason pulled a chair over to the bed and sat down. At that point Mary entered with a tray bearing a coffee pot and two cups.

''Just leave the tray, Mary,'' Milo said.

''I've got to hold your cup—''

''Carl will help me with my coffee, won't you, boy?'' Milo asked.

''Sure, Sheriff.''

''See? Just leave the tray, Mary. Go get some rest.

You must be tired of waiting on me hand and foot.''

''Hmph,'' she said. She put the tray down and left.

''That woman is a saint, isn't she?'' Milo asked.

''Uh—''

''I was being sarcastic, Carl. Never mind. Pour the coffee and tell me your problem.''

Mason poured two cups and held the sheriff's to his mouth whenever he wanted a sip. In between sips he told the man his problem.

''Well,'' Milo said, ''this is an easy one to solve.''

''It is?''

''Sure,'' the sheriff said. ''If you don't want to get killed, don't go.''

''But . . . somebody's got to go.''

''Let Adams do it.''

''But . . . he ain't a lawman. He's doing it for revenge.''

''What the hell is the difference why he's doing it?'' Milo said. ''He's good at it, he's got a reputation for it. Let him do it himself.''

Mason put his coffee cup down.

''Why the long face?''

''I wouldn't feel right,'' Mason said. ''I mean, what if he got killed and I could have helped him?''

''You mean like Jennings? The shotgun for the stage?'' Milo asked.

''Exactly like him,'' Mason said. Then he squared his shoulders. ''No, I got to go with him, Sheriff. I can't be like Jennings. I mean, what if the gang comes back to town and kills some more of our people?''

''Not much chance of that, son,'' Milo said. ''But it sounds to me like you just made up your mind.''

Mason stared at the sheriff and said, "Yeah, I did, didn't I?"

"Open that drawer," Milo said, pointing to the night table on his side of the bed.

Mason opened it.

"Look inside."

Mason did. There were a few bedside items, but the one he noticed the most was Milo's badge.

"Take out the badge."

Mason did so.

"Wear that when you go," Milo said.

"Wear your badge?"

"It's yours now," Milo said. "At least until I get back on my feet."

"Gee, Sheriff, I don't know—"

"Come on. Put that deputy's badge in the drawer and pin that one on."

Mason hesitated, and then did as he was told. When he closed the drawer with the deputy's badge in it, he was wearing the sheriff's star.

"Carl," Milo said, "I'm gonna tell you something I ain't never told anybody."

"What's that, Sheriff?"

"I ain't a very good lawman, Carl," Milo said. "That's how I got myself shot up, and most of my posse killed—by not being a very good lawman."

"But Sheriff—"

"No buts," Milo said. "If you pull this off, boy, if you catch that gang and bring back the money, you'll be a better lawman than I ever was, or could be. You'll be wearing that badge for good."

"I don't want to take your job, Sheriff."

"Well, I want you to take it," Milo said. "I'm damn tired of doing a job I don't like and one I'm not very good at."

"I—I don't know what to say."

"Don't say anything, Carl," Milo said. "Just go and do what a lawman is supposed to do."

Mason got up and walked to the door, stopped there, and turned, as if to say something.

"Make me proud, boy," Milo said. "But do me a favor."

"What's that?"

"Don't get yourself killed."

"I'll try not to."

THIRTY-FOUR

When Mason went downstairs, Mary Milo was waiting for him.

"Finished already?" she asked.

"Yes."

"I'll walk you to the door."

They went to the front door together, but instead of opening it for him, she leaned against him. The feel of her body was familiar and unsettling. He felt himself beginning to react.

"I've missed you, Carl," she whispered.

"Mary," he said, "this is not a good idea."

She ran her hands up his arms and said, "You used to think it was a very good idea."

"I was wrong."

"It wasn't good?"

"No, I meant . . . I mean, it was good, but . . . it's not a good idea now."

He could feel her nails digging into him through his shirt.

"I haven't been with anyone since you, Carl," she said, digging into his arms even harder. "Not with Quint, not with anyone."

"Mary," Mason said, easing away from her, "I have to go. I've got work to do."

Suddenly she turned cold and backed away from him, arms folded beneath her round, peach-sized breasts.

"Go, then," she said. "Who needs you? There are plenty of men in town."

"Mary," he said, "you have a husband."

"That didn't used to bother you, Carl."

"Well," he said, "to tell you the truth, it does now."

"When did you become such a coward, Carl?"

Mason ignored the question and said, "I have to go."

He went out the door with her words echoing in his ears: "Go! Who needs you! Who needs you!"

After Mason left, Mary Milo went upstairs to talk to her husband.

"So what's Carl up to?" she asked, collecting the tray from the night table.

"He's gonna go after the Borton Boys."

She stared at him.

"*He* is?" she asked. "Quint, he's just a boy."

"He's not a boy," Milo said, "he's a man. He's gonna make a better lawman than I ever did."

"If he doesn't get killed."

"He won't."

"Does he have a posse?"

"No," Milo said, "there won't be any more posses

from this town. Not after what happened to the last one.''

"Then he will get himself killed if he goes up against them alone."

"He won't be alone," Milo said. "He'll have one man with him."

"And one man will make a difference?" she asked.

"It will when that one man is Clint Adams."

"The Gunsmith?"

"That's him."

"Why is he getting involved?"

"Apparently," Milo said, "he knew the woman who was on the stage, the one that was killed."

"The way I hear it," Mary said, "he's know lots of women."

Sleepily, Milo said, "I guess that's part of his reputation, all right."

Mary watched as her husband's eyes closed and he drifted off to sleep.

She left the room with the tray, thinking that was one part of the man's reputation she could check out for herself.

THIRTY-FIVE

While Clint was eating breakfast the next morning, Deputy Carl Mason came walking in. He spotted Clint, who waved him over.

"I was just finishing up," Clint said. "Want to take a walk?"

"Sure."

Clint paid the bill, and the two men went outside and started to walk, slowly.

"You look like a man who's come to a decision," Clint said.

"It shows, huh? Well, yeah, you're right."

"Am I going after these Bortons alone?"

"Would you?" Mason asked. "Would you go alone if I told you I decided not to go?"

"Yes."

"Against all five?"

"Yes," Clint said, again, and then added, "who says I have to face all five of them at one time?"

"You mean separate them?"

"They've got to be apart sometime."

"I guess so," Mason said, rubbing his hairless jaw. Clint doubted that the young man could have grown a beard if he wanted to.

"So?" Clint asked.

"Oh," Mason said, "I'm going, all right. I owe it to that dead woman, and to the town, and to the sheriff for giving me this job."

"When?"

"What?"

"When did he give you this job?"

"Over a year ago."

"And no experience before that?"

"No, sir."

Clint frowned.

"You're worried, aren't you?" the deputy said. "That I won't be able to pull my own weight."

"Whether you can or not, I need you with me," Clint said. He pointed to the young man's chest. "You're the sheriff, now. I need your official standing to back me up even more than I need your gun."

"I can use my gun, Mr. Adams."

"Well, that's good, because you're going to have to."

"I can show you," Mason went on. "We can go somewhere, and I could show you."

Clint thought a moment and then said, "Sure, why not? Let's go someplace and you can show me what you've got."

They went to a clearing outside of town, where it looked like someone had already practiced many times before.

"Why do I feel like I've been had?" Clint asked.

"Okay," Mason said, "I do shoot out here from time to time."

"From the ruts worn into the ground I'd say more than time to time."

Mason nodded and said, "A lot."

Clint looked over at a two-by-four that had been suspended between two rocks. On the two-by-four were balanced some bottles and cans.

"You shoot at those?" he asked.

"Yes, sir."

"Hit what you shoot at?"

"Most of the time."

"What's most of the time?" Clint asked. "Six times out of ten? Seven out of ten? Nine out of ten?"

"Eight," Mason said, "eight times out of ten."

"Why only eight?" Clint asked. "Why not ten out of ten?"

"That'd be perfect," Mason said. "Nobody's perfect."

Clint turned, drew his gun and snapped off five shots—only five, because the chamber beneath the hammer had been empty. Two bottles shattered, and three cans flew off the board. He reloaded immediately—six shells, this time—and fired six more times. Each time a bottle shattered or a can went flying. When his tenth shot sent a can flying in the air he fired his last bullet at it, striking it before it could hit the ground.

"Jesus!" Mason said.

Clint reloaded and holstered his gun.

"I ain't never seen anything like that."

"And I'm not the only man who can do it," Clint

said, folding his arms. "There are others, and if you're not perfect, you've got to hope you never run into some-one who is."

"Okay," Mason said, "I get your point—but the Bor-ton Boys aren't perfect."

"What makes you say that?"

"Because they didn't get away clean after they robbed the bank," Mason explained, "and they didn't get to the safe."

"Wait, say that again?"

"They didn't get away—"

"No, the other part."

"They never got into the safe."

"That's it!" Clint said.

"That's what?"

"The safe," Clint said. "Ben Borton has several rep-utations. One is with a gun. He supposed to be very good with a gun."

"Fast?"

"Fast and a dead shot."

"Is he perfect?"

"I don't know," Clint said, "I've never run across him."

"What's his other reputation?"

"He's got a huge ego," Clint said. "He's not going to leave this area without getting into that safe, no matter how many of his brothers get shot up."

Mason looked shocked.

"You think they're gonna come back?"

"I sure do," Clint said, "and I'll tell you why. It's because they think you'd never expect that."

"They're right," Mason said, "I never would."

"I never heard that they didn't get the safe," Clint said. "God, it's so simple."

"What makes you think they'd try it? It sounds so crazy."

"And that's the other reputation Ben Borton has," Clint said.

"What?"

"They say he's crazy."

THIRTY-SIX

Clint and Mason went back to town to talk to the bank manager.

"They killed the manager," Mason said, "but his brother was head teller, and now he's the manager."

"Convenient," Clint said.

They entered the bank, and Mason went to talk to the pretty teller who had been terrorized by Griff Borton.

"Sally, would you tell Sam that we'd like to see him?" Mason asked.

Sally looked over Mason's shoulder at Clint, her eyes showing fright.

"Don't worry," Mason said. "He's with me. His name is Clint Adams—or maybe you heard of him as the Gunsmith?"

Now her eyes widened, and she said, "I have heard of him. I'll tell Mr. Gateway you're here."

She left her window, went and knocked on the manager's door, and went inside. She was back in seconds.

"You can go in."

"Thanks, Sally," Mason said.

"Thank you, Ma'am," Clint said, tipping his hat. He found her an inordinately pretty woman to be cooped up in a bank. Rich chestnut hair was done up behind her head, and when she let it down he knew it would trail more than halfway down her back. If it was let down in front it would hide her breasts like a curtain of silk, allowing just a hint of what was behind it to show through.

"Clint?" Mason said.

"Hmmm? Oh, yeah, sure. Let's go."

They went inside and closed the door.

Once they were inside, Sally retook her position behind her teller's window, but she couldn't keep still. There was something about the way Clint Adams looked, and the way he looked *at* her, that was making her fidget. She couldn't figure out what it was, and then she realized that she was excited, *sexually* excited.

She quickly looked around to see if anyone noticed.

"Gentleman, what can I do for you?" Samuel Gateway asked.

His clothing was much better than those he had worn when he was *just* head teller. He was now wearing clothes befitting his position.

"Sam, this is Clint Adams," Mason said. "Clint, Sam Gateway, the manager. His brother, Horace, was killed in the robbery."

"My sympathies," Clint said.

"Thank you, thank you, but there's no point in dwelling on the dead. There's too much living to be done, eh?''

"I suppose so.''

Clint had no brothers, but he remembered Wyatt Earp's grief over losing one, and saw none of that in this man's eyes.

"What can I do for you gentlemen?'' he asked.

"Empty out your safe," Clint said.

"W-what?'' Gateway said, immediately looking frightened. Was he going to be robbed by the law?

"Let me explain, Sam," Mason said. "Mr. Adams believes that the bank robbers are going to come back for the contents of the safe.''

"B-but that would be foolhardy.''

"It's the last thing you'd expect, isn't it?'' Clint asked.

"Why, yes, it is.''

"That's why they'll do it.''

Gateway was drywashing his hands nervously.

"What am I to do, then?''

"Take the contents of the safe and put them somewhere else," Clint said.

"But . . . where?''

Mason and Gateway both looked to Clint for the answer to that question.

"Well," Clint said, "how about the jail? We could put the money in a cell and lock it.''

"And who will have the key?'' Gateway asked.

"Why, you will, Mr. Gateway," Clint said. "After all, aren't you the bank manager now that your brother is . . . dead?''

"Well, yes, of course I am.''

"What do you think, Carl?" Clint asked the acting sheriff.

"Well," Mason said, "I've gone along with you this far. Why not?"

"All right," Clint said. "Now the only question is how to transfer the money without attracting a lot of attention."

"At night," Mason said. "We'll have to move the money at night."

"Mr. Gateway," Clint said, "can you meet us here after dark?"

"Tonight?" Gateway asked. "You want to do it tonight?"

"Well," Clint said, "they might show up here tomorrow. I think we should make sure the money is safe, don't you?"

"Of course, of course," Gateway said. "Very well, I'll meet you. Uh, at what time?"

"Midnight?" Mason asked Clint.

"Let's make it three," Clint said. "The only people on the street then should be drunks who can't see straight, anyway."

"All right," Mason said, "three A.M. it is." He looked at Gateway. "Meet you at three?"

"I—I'll be here."

"Thanks for the cooperation, Sam," Mason said.

"Well . . . thank you for safeguarding the bank's money."

"You mean the town's money, don't you?" Clint asked.

"Yes, yes, of course," Gateway said, hurriedly, "the town's money."

"We'll see you later, Mr. Gateway," Clint said. "You're being very smart to go along with us."

"I hope so," Gateway said. "After all, this is just a hunch on your part, isn't it?"

"Better to be safe than sorry, eh?" Clint asked.

At that point, he and Mason turned and left the office. Outside, the pretty teller felt her eyes once again drawn to Clint. He saw her looking and smiled, and she turned away in response.

Outside the bank the two men stopped.

"Something's bothering me," Clint said.

"What?"

"Well, that man doesn't seem too broken up about having his brother killed."

"Maybe he just doesn't want to show it."

"How well did you know his brother?"

"Not well at all."

"And what about him?"

"Not well, either."

"You call him by his first name."

"Only because I bank here and see him almost every day—that is, I did see him often when he was head teller. I suppose I won't be seeing him much of him now that he's manager."

"How did he feel about that?" Clint asked.

"About what?"

"About his brother being manager and him being head teller."

"I don't know," Mason said. "They're brothers, what did it matter who was bank manager?"

"Do you have any brothers?" Clint asked.

"No."

"Neither do I," Clint said, "but I know some pretty close brothers, like the Earps and the Mastersons—hell, even the James boys showed how they felt about each other. This man is kind of cold about his brother's death."

"Hey," Mason said, "everybody grieves in their own way."

"I know all about that," Clint said. "It just doesn't sit right with me, is all."

"We better get some rest," Mason said, "if we're gonna be back here at three A.M."

"You're right," Clint said. "I'll see you at your office about a quarter to three."

"I'll be there."

The two men split up and went their separate ways.

THIRTY-SEVEN

Clint was wondering what to do while he waited for a quarter to three to roll around when there was a knock on his door. He palmed his gun and carried it to the door with him. Would the Bortons knock on his door and shoot him when he opened it?

"Who is it?"

There was a moment's hesitation on the other side of the door, and then a woman said, "It's Mary Milo. I— I'm the sheriff's wife."

"The sheriff's—" Clint opened the door. "Is he all right?"

"Oh, hello," she said, blinking rapidly, as if surprised to see him.

She was blond, in her early to mid-thirties, and very pretty. Her body looked long and lean, with small but solid breasts.

"I, uh, are you Mr. Adams?"

"That's right."

"May I come in?"

"It's late, Mrs. Milo. Is there something I can do for you?"

She was wearing a shawl, and now she let it slip off her shoulders just a bit. It wasn't much, but it was a suggestive move. Clint realized that she had the look. He had seen it before in women who were dissatisfied with their lot in life. Women who were looking outside their marriage for something they couldn't get inside of it.

Or maybe he was reading a lot into a simple slip of a shawl.

"Ma'am—"

"Please," she said, "call me Mary. May I come in . . . just for a little while?"

"Well . . . I suppose . . ."

He backed away to allow her to enter, and that was when she saw the gun.

"Do you make a habit of answering the door with your gun?" she asked.

"Yes," he answered, "I do."

"Well, I don't think you'll be needing it for me, will you?"

"I don't suppose I will. Would you close the door, please?"

She closed the door, and he replaced his gun in the holster on the bedpost.

"Were you asleep?" she asked, looking at the rumpled bed.

"No, I was just sitting . . . thinking."

"I like a man who thinks."

"Mrs. Milo," he said, "what brings you here?"

"Well, to be truthful," she said, "your reputation."

"My reputation with a gun brought you here to-night?" he asked.

"Well, no . . . your other reputation . . . with women."

No, he thought, no doubt about it, at all.

"Mrs. Milo—"

"I asked you to call me Mary."

"Mrs. Milo, I don't know you at all—"

"We can get acquainted, then."

"I don't think—"

"Do aggressive women bother you, Mr. Adams?"

Now the shawl dropped to the floor. No question about it, now. She was looking for something he really didn't want to give her.

"Aggressive *married* women bother me," he said.

"Oh, that," she said. "Quint and I haven't been a married couple for a long time. In fact, I don't even think he'd care that I'm here."

"I care."

"Well," she said, her hands drifting to the buttons at the front of her dress, "you finally said something nice."

"No," he said, "I didn't mean it as something nice. I mean, I care that you're here and that you're legally married."

"Don't let that stop you," she said. "I've been real curious about you ever since I heard you were in town. I've heard women say you're irresistible."

"That's not true," Clint said. "I'm very resistable."

"I've heard that you know how to make a woman feel like a woman."

"You can't believe everything you hear, Mrs. Milo."

"Are you going to call me Mary, or not?"

"I think not."

"Well, maybe this will help loosen you up."

In a jiffy she had the buttons of her dress undone and peeled it down to her waist. She was wearing no undergarment, and her breasts were absolutely beautiful, about the size of ripe peaches, firm and pink tipped. He felt his mouth go dry, but he was determined not to get involved with the sheriff's wife, no matter how tempting she was.

And she was tempting . . .

"Put your dress back on, Mrs. Milo," he said, sternly, trying not to show that her nakedness affected him. "This is not going to happen."

"It's not?" she asked, with a pout.

"I'm sorry," he said, "but no."

She stood there staring at him for a few moments, and then all signs of flirtation and coquettishness disappeared.

"Fine," she said, pulling her dress up, "but you don't know what you're missing."

"I'm sure you're right."

"Just ask Carl," she said. "He'll tell you."

"Carl . . . Mason? The deputy?"

"That's right," she said. "Only he rejected me long ago, and again today. You know, this could affect a woman's self-esteem."

Clint watched as she buttoned her dress, and then he picked up her shawl and handed it to her.

"Mrs. Milo," he said, and then, "Mary, I don't think

you have a self-esteem problem at all—and I don't think you need to."

"Well," she said, taking the shawl, "now that was something nice, wasn't it?"

"Yes, Ma'am," he said, "that was something nice."

"Well, I guess I'll have to be satisfied with that," she said, turning toward the door. "Just tell me one thing before I go."

"What's that?"

"Are you as good as they say?"

He knew what she meant—was he as good as she'd heard women say he was.

He smiled, just a bit meanly, and said, "You don't know what you're missing."

She sighed and said, "That's what I was afraid of," and left.

THIRTY-EIGHT

After she left, he felt foolish for that last comment. He didn't know where she had gotten her information, but he *had* been with a lot of women over the years—he *loved* women—and he supposed some of them might have talked about him to other women.

Sometimes his own body's weakness annoyed him, though. His body reacted on its own to beautiful women, and Mary Milo had certainly been that, standing there with her dress half-off and her pale skin and pink-tipped globes. He was still hard just thinking about her, so he knew he was going to have to stop.

He sat back down on the bed, once again wondering what to do until it was time to meet with the deputy— or, the *acting* sheriff. But he also needed to find something to take his mind off Mary Milo so that he wouldn't keep replaying the way she looked in his head.

He'd told her that it was late, but it actually wasn't. On any normal day Clint would not even be in his room at this time of the evening. He'd be at a saloon, drinking, talking, or playing poker. So he decided to go out. That would take his mind off the woman who had offered herself to him, and hopefully his body would calm down.

Clint left the hotel and decided that instead of going to a saloon he'd go to Papa John's for something to eat. On his way there he remembered that he wanted to buy Kate a headstone. He also remembered that he didn't know her last name. What was he going to have written on the stone? "Here lies Kate"? He felt miserable about what had happened to her after he left her. It wasn't his fault—it was the fault of the Bortons—but he still felt a little responsible.

Think about something else, he told himself. All right, then, the bank manager, Gateway. Not at all the picture of a grieving brother, and that bothered him. The man seemed all too satisfied with his lot in life, even though it had come at the expense of his brother's life. Not natural, Clint thought, not natural at all.

As he entered Papa John's, the proprietor came rushing over to him, rubbing his meaty hands together.

"You decided to come back."

"Yes."

"Good, good. Uh, the lady is not with you tonight?"

"The lady . . . has moved on."

"Ah, I see."

At that moment, Clint spotted the pretty bank teller, Sally, sitting alone at a table.

"The lady from the bank," Clint said.

"You mean Sally?"

"Yes," Clint said. "Has she already eaten?"

"She has just now ordered," Papa John said. "I must seat you and then go and prepare her food."

"I'll have the same thing she's having."

"Very good."

"And bring both plates to the same table," he said. "And some coffee."

"Ah, you know her?"

"No," Clint said, "but I'm about to."

Papa John went into the kitchen, and Clint walked over to Sally's table. The place was less than half full, and none of the tables immediately surrounding Sally were occupied. Clint sat at the table right next to her.

"Well, hello," he said.

She had been sitting with her eyes on the tabletop, lost in thought. At the sound of his voice she turned and was startled. He had no way of knowing it, but she'd been thinking about him at that precise moment.

"Remember me?" he asked.

"From the bank, right?" she asked, hoping her voice wouldn't give away her nervousness.

"That's right," he said. "Clint Adams."

"Yes, Mr. Adams."

"And you're Sally, right?"

"That's right." Apparently, he had gone to the trouble of finding out her name. For some reason that made her feel good. "Sally Mills."

"Well, Sally Mills," he said, "to tell you the truth, I hate eating alone, and since you and I know each other—"

"Oh, Mr. Adams," she said, "we hardly know each other at all."

"Well," he said, "I know you better than I know any of these other people."

She stifled a laugh and said, "That's true."

"And I don't want to eat with them," he said. "I'd like to eat with you, and then we could get to know each other. What do you say?"

"Well . . ." she said, hesitantly. She was afraid that if he sat at the same table with her she would make a fool of herself. "All right." She decided to be bold.

"Thank you," he said, and moved to join her, sitting right across from her.

At that moment Papa John appeared with a pot of coffee and two cups. He set them down on the table with a smile and returned to the kitchen.

"Mr. Adams," she said, scolding him. "You had this planned."

"Yes, Ma'am," he said. "As soon as I walked in the door I planned it. Do you mind?"

"No," she said, with a sigh. "No, I don't suppose I mind at all."

THIRTY-NINE

She told him that she was born in the town of Tierney and expected to die there—probably in her cage at the bank when she was in her sixties or seventies.

"Why not leave?"

"It's my home," she said. "All I've ever known."

"Wouldn't you like to see the rest of the country?" he asked. "Maybe the rest of the world?"

"That would take a lot of money," she said. "On my salary I can't even save that much."

"What you need to do is meet a rich man."

She laughed and said, "Well, working in a bank would certainly come in handy for that."

Over a dessert of peach pie he said, "Sally, can I ask you something?"

"Of course," she said. "We're friends now, aren't we?" She felt *much* more comfortable with him than she had ever thought she could be with any man. "What is it?"

"The day of the robbery," he said. "Do you remember it?"

Her face fell, and she said, "Vividly. The way that man shot down Mr. and Mrs. Andrews was horrible."

"And Mr. Gateway?" Clint asked. "He was shot, too, wasn't he?"

"He was, yes . . ." she said, thoughtfully, "but to tell you the truth, I didn't see which robber shot him."

"What did you see?"

"I just saw Mr. Gateway—Samuel, that is—leaning over his brother, yelling that they had shot him."

"But you did see the robbers shoot the couple down?" Clint asked.

"Yes, clear as day," she said. "I could identify the man, and I will, if he's ever caught."

"Sally, how is Samuel Gateway to work for?" he asked. "Better or worse than Horace?"

"Oh, my Lord, Samuel is a tyrant. He was as head teller and he's even worse as manager. The other Mr. Gateway was a sweetheart."

"I see."

"Why are you interested in all this?"

"I'm just trying to put something together in my head," he said. "Samuel doesn't seem all that broken up about Horace's death."

Sally leaned closer and said in a low voice, "Between you and me, he's not."

"Really?"

"Yes," she said, sitting back. "They argued all the time."

"About what?"

"Samuel thought he should be manager and Horace

should be head teller. He said that Horace didn't have any business sense.''

''Why was that?''

''Mr. Gateway—Horace—took it easy on people who owed the bank money, and he was too generous with loans. At least, that's what Samuel always said.''

''So Horace's death really gave Samuel what he wanted,'' Clint said.

''I suppose so,'' she said, ''although I wouldn't say he was *happy* about it. I'm sure he would have liked to have gotten the job another way.''

''Maybe,'' Clint said, ''there was no other way.''

''What do you mean?''

''Oh, nothing,'' Clint said. ''I'm just thinking out loud.''

He stared across the table at Sally. She was not as beautiful as Mary Milo, but she was very pretty, younger, and fresher looking—and not married.

''Would you like to go for a walk?''

''It's dark out.''

''I'll protect you,'' he promised.

She hesitated a moment and then said, ''All right.''

FORTY

"Do you always move this fast?" she asked later, as they lay in bed in his hotel room together.

"No," he said, "but I felt a sense of urgency with you. You see, I don't know how long I'll be here."

She had been lying with her head on his shoulder and now she turned onto her back, pulling the sheet up to her neck.

"I can't believe I did this," she said. "This is so unlike me."

"Are you sorry?"

"Sorry? No, not at all. In fact I'm . . . well, thrilled! I mean, I have been with men before, but it had never been this good. In fact, I thought that when I got married this part of it would be a . . . chore. Now I know it doesn't have to be, and I have you to thank for it. How could I be sorry?"

"That's good," he said. "I only wanted it to be nice."

"Well, I've had three lovers other than you," she said, frankly, "and they only wanted it to be nice for them."

"They were fools," he said.

Clint had not even suggested that they go to his hotel. They simply walked to it from Papa John's. Once in the room he disrobed her, peeling off layers until she was naked, and nervous.

"Relax," he told her, just lightly brushing her nipples with his palms. She had small but exquisite breasts, was as pale as Mary Milo had been, but had brown nipples rather than pink. Her hair was too dark to be blond and too light to be black. Chestnut was all he could think of.

Once she was naked, he reached for her hair and took it down. As he had suspected, it fell past her shoulders in shimmering waves.

"I'm just a little nervous," she admitted.

"It'll pass," he said, "I promise."

And it did.

Tentatively, she returned the favor, undressing him. When they were both naked they crawled into bed together. Once there, with their bodies pressed together, all nervousness fled. She may not have had many lovers, but she made up in energy what she might have lacked in experience. And when he kissed his way from her nipples to the tangle of hair between her legs, she tensed up and held his head there, babbling incoherent words.

Now, as they lay side by side, Clint wondered what time it was. Nowhere close to three, surely, but he didn't want to lose track, and with Sally in bed with him, he might have. He felt slightly guilty for, at one point in the dark, having fantasized that he was in bed with Mary Milo and not Sally. However, it had only lasted for an instant, and then he gave his entire attention to Miss Sally Mills.

"What are you thinking?" she asked.

"I have something to do later."

"We don't have all night?"

"If you stay," he said, "I have to go out around two-thirty, but I shouldn't be long."

"Are you asking me to stay?"

"Yes."

"Then I'll be here."

He turned, bent over her and kissed her, meaning it more as a goodnight kiss, but it quickly turned into something else, something more passionate, almost violent . . .

"This time," she whispered against his mouth, "I want to go wild."

He wouldn't have guessed she had *that* kind of streak in her.

FORTY-ONE

When Clint reached the sheriff's office, "acting" Sheriff Mason was ready to go. For just a moment Clint toyed with the idea of mentioning what had happened with Mary Milo, but if the deputy had, indeed, had a relationship with the woman, he didn't think it would be wise, so he kept quiet.

"Ready?" he asked.

"I'm ready," Mason said, "but I was thinking about something."

"What?"

"What if the two of us can't handle what's in the safe?" he asked. "I mean, we don't want to have to make more than one trip from the bank to here."

"No, you're right," Clint said, "we don't. Well, if we have a choice, we'll just have to move all the cash. This is a small town, though, so how much could there be?"

"Sam says they got five thousand the first time—and

152

that was just from the tellers' cages. Of course, it was a pay day for a lot of the ranchhands in the area.''

"Aren't they paid in cash?" Clint asked.

"Still, they come to the bank. That's what the young couple, the Andrews, who were killed were doing there.''

"Well then, let's get over there and see what we're dealing with.''

When they reached the bank, the street was deserted. From farther down the street they heard the strains of a saloon piano, played with more enthusiasm than skill. Clint knocked on the door, and within moments Sam Gateway opened it for them.

"Come in, gentlemen," he said, backing away so they could enter. Clint came in last and closed the door behind him, making sure it was locked.

"Are you alone, Sam?" Mason asked.

"Yes," the manager said, "I didn't want to bring anyone else in on this. The fewer people who know about it, the better.''

"My feelings exactly," Clint said, which was why he hadn't told Sally Mills where he was going.

"Is the safe open?" Mason asked.

"Not yet," Sam said. "If you'll wait here, I'll open it.''

He went behind the tellers' cages to the safe, which was a walk-in. Clint wondered why a town this small had such a safe. He walked over to the teller cages but stayed on his side.

"Mr. Gateway?"

"Hmmm?" Gateway said, as he entered the combination to the safe.

"Can you tell me which of the Borton Boys shot your brother?"

Gateway stopped and looked over his shoulder at Clint.

"Why do you want to know that?"

"I'm just trying to piece things together," Clint said. Mason was watching him carefully.

"Well," Gateway said, abandoning the safe for a moment, "I can't rightly say. Once the shooting started—"

"Well, from what I understand," Clint said, interrupting him, "one robber shot the man and another shot the woman. Was it one of them who then shot your brother? Or was he shot first?"

"It all happened so fast," Gateway said. "I'm afraid I couldn't tell you."

"I see. Okay, let's get that safe open. Sorry I interrupted you."

"Now I'll have to start all over," Gateway groused.

"That's okay," Clint said. "We have time."

Gateway finally got the door open and swung it wide.

"What's in there?" Mason asked.

"Mostly cash."

"All we want is the cash," Mason said. "Do you have any sacks?"

"I have money bags—"

"We don't want to use them," Clint said. "Just in case anyone is around at this time of night, we don't want them to know what we're carrying. Do you have any plain sacks? Gunny sacks or canvas sacks?"

"I think we have some canvas sacks in the back."

"Take me there," Clint said.

He followed Gateway to the rear of the bank, purposely crowding the man.

"You know, this still bothers me about your brother," he said.

"I don't see why," Gateway said. "Dead is dead."

"Were you and he close?"

There was a moment's hesitation, and then Gateway said, "Yes, we were extremely close."

"Even though he was in a position of authority?"

"I think I answered that once before," Gateway said. "That's just the way it happened."

"Was he a good bank manager?"

"He was fair," Gateway said. "Sometimes too fair, and too loose with the bank's money."

"You mean for loans?"

"Loans, mortgages," Gateway said. "He let many of his 'neighbors' put off their payments for too long when he should have called in a loan or foreclosed on a property."

"I see," Clint said, "and you're not like that?"

"No, Mr. Adams," Gateway said, "I'm not. Here are the bags."

Clint bent over and picked them up. He didn't know what had come in them, but there were four of them and they were a good size.

"Will all the cash fit in these?" he asked.

"Probably three of them would carry it all."

"We'll take the fourth, just in case."

Clint carried the bags and followed Gateway back to the front of the bank. The smaller man was walking quickly, as if trying to stay ahead of Clint and his questions.

When they reached the front of the bank, the three of them set about dumping the cash into the bags. In the end, they had to use the fourth bag, filling it halfway.

"How much is here?" Clint asked.

"In excess of forty thousand," Gateway said.

"That's a big responsibility," Clint said.

"And now, I am afraid, it is yours," the bank manager said.

"Well, you'll have the key to the cell, Mr. Gateway," Mason said.

"Is there another key, Deputy?"

"No, sir," Mason said. "Once we lock that money in a cell, you're the only one with a key—so I'll ask you not to lose it."

"I'll make you a deal, Deputy."

"What's that?"

"You don't lose my money," Gateway said, "and I won't lose your key."

FORTY-TWO

They let Gateway go out first and look up and down the street. When he reported that the street was empty, they came out, each carrying two sacks. Gateway locked the bank door behind them.

It struck Clint that at that moment they were extremely vulnerable. If anyone had known about this exchange of money from the bank to the jail they could catch both men with their hands full, and with no access to their guns.

"Mr. Gateway?" Clint said. "I wonder if you'd take out my gun and hold on to it, just in case."

"I have my own, Mr. Adams," the man said, taking a cut-down Colt from inside his jacket.

"Do you always carry that?"

"Yes, sir."

The unspoken question hung in the air between them: why had he not used it during the robbery?

157

"All right, then, sir," Clint said, "just hold on to it and stay alert."

"I will."

They made their way across the street to the sheriff's office with no fuss or fanfare. Gateway opened the door for them, and they carried the sacks to one of the cells and put them down right in the center.

"There," Mason said.

They left the cell. Mason locked it, turned, and gave the key to Gateway, who was still holding his gun.

"You can put that away now, Sam," Mason said.

"May I see that gun?"

"Why?" Gateway asked.

"Well, I am a gunsmith. The workmanship looks interesting."

Gateway hesitated, and then said, "Well, all right."

He handed the gun over to Clint, who turned it over in his hands. It was singularly unremarkable, but he made a show of studying it. When he lifted it to his face to sight down the barrel, he sniffed and then returned the gun to Sam Gateway.

"Very nice. Did you cut it down yourself?"

"No, I had it done for me."

"The man did a good job."

"I'm glad to hear that," Gateway said, and put the gun away.

"Well, Sam," Mason said, "your bank's money is safe. I guess you can go home to sleep."

"Where do you live?" Clint asked.

"The north end of town, in a house."

"Ah, is the house supplied by the bank?"

"Why, yes it is."

"That means it was your brother's house?"

"It was, yes," Gateway said, "and now it's mine."

Clint could see that the little man was starting to become agitated by all the questions, so Clint decided to stop—for the time being.

"Okay, Mr. Gateway," Clint said, "good night, sir."

"Good night to both of you," Gateway said, "and thank you again for the service you're doing for the bank."

"For the town, Sam," Mason said.

"Yes, certainly," Gateway said, "for the town."

They waited until Gateway left, and then Mason turned to face Clint.

"Why all the questions about his brother?"

"I told you something didn't sit right with me. Sally Olson told me she saw the robbers shoot the Andrews couple. But she didn't see any of them shoot the manager."

"So you think Sam shot his own brother?"

Clint didn't answer.

"You do," Mason said, incredulously. "You do think he took the opportunity to shoot his own brother and take his job?"

"It's possible," Clint said. "He does carry a gun, and it has been fired recently. I could smell it. Also, why didn't he use the gun to try to stop the robbery?"

"I don't know."

"Maybe it was because he had a better use for it."

"Well," Mason asked, "how do we prove something like this?"

"Two ways," Clint said. "If he confesses . . ."

"Yeah."

"Or we could ask the Bortons, when we catch them."

FORTY-THREE

Ben Borton awoke the next morning excited. He was wrapped in blanket with Belle, her big body keeping him warm all night.

He looked over at Jake, who was in his own blanket with the new girl, Bridget. During their conversation about Belle riding into town with them they had all forgotten about the girl. When they remembered she was there, it was Jake who went over to talk to her, who then came back to Ben.

"She says she's in," Jake said. "She'll watch over Will while we're gone."

"Can we trust her?" Ben asked.

"She says it was the best day of her life when we came to her farm," Jake said. "I think we can trust her."

"Let's make sure," Ben said.

That was when they took her. They spread out a blanket and she got down on her back, her head in Belle's lap. First Ben, then Jake, then Ted. Griff wanted a turn, but because of his wound, she had to get on top of him, supporting most of her weight with her legs so as not to put too much pressure on him. After that, Ben had her again, and the initiation was over.

She was in the Borton gang.

"Are you awake?" Belle asked.

"Yes," Ben said. He was lying behind her, spoon fashion, his thick penis wedged into the crack between her buttocks. It was a very comfortable position, and he hated to move from it, but it was time.

"Do you want to do it before breakfast?" she asked.

"No," he said. "Go ahead and get breakfast, and then we'll go into town and make our withdrawal"

Belle sighed. She liked sex in the morning, but Ben—and all the Borton Boys—liked it when they liked it, when the feeling hit them.

She tossed back the blanket and stood up naked. Ben looked at her chunky breasts and thighs and watched the muscles bunch in her buttocks as she moved around. She grabbed a peasant blouse and skirt, and he said, "Dress for riding, Belle."

"Oh, right."

She changed into a pair of jeans and a man's shirt and then went to the fire to start breakfast.

Ben looked over to where Bridget was crawling from the blanket she'd shared with Jake. She was naked, with lovely skin but small breasts and an almost boyish butt. She would fill out, though, over time. The young ones trained well, he'd learned that from Baby.

They'd buried Baby away from the camp. That was something else they owed to the town of Tierney. Ben hoped that the sheriff would try to stop them today—that is, providing he was still alive.

He rolled out of the blanket, stood up, and stretched, and then picked up his gunbelt and strapped it on. Jake did the same and then came over to him.

"How was she?" Ben asked.

"She was no virgin before we had her," Jake said. "She was all right. She'll learn."

Ted approached, wearing his gun.

"When do we leave?"

"Right after breakfast," Ben said. "We'll need a good one, because we don't know when we'll be able to stop for lunch."

"What should we do before we go?" Ted asked.

"Let's get Will into the buckboard," Ben said. "We might have to move fast when we get back here."

"And Griff?" Jake asked.

"Griff's gonna try to sit a horse," Ben said. "We'll need his gun."

"I'm still not sure this is a good idea, Ben," Ted said.

"Well," Ben said, "lucky we're not voting on it, then, isn't it? I'm going down to the creek to wash my face."

Jake and Ted watched their older brother walk out of camp toward the creek.

"What do you think of this, Jake?" Ted asked.

"I think Ben has never steered us wrong so far," Jake said. "If he wants to do this, I'm with him."

"Oh, I am, too," Ted said. "I'm just wondering . . ."

"Wondering what?"

"About going back to a town that we just hit," Ted said.

"It's just the kind of thing Ben would do, don't ya think?"

"I guess that's why people say he's crazy."

"Yeah," Jake said, "crazy like a fox—but don't ever let him hear you say it."

"I won't," Ted said. "I ain't that stupid."

The smell of coffee filled the air, and both men turned toward the source.

"Coffee's ready," Belle said.

"Come on," Jake said. "One quick cup and then we'll get Will into the buckboard."

After getting their younger brother into the buckboard and making him as comfortable as they could, the brothers and Belle collected their guns and saddled their horses.

"How we gonna do this, Ben?" Ted asked. "People are gonna recognize us when we ride in."

"You think anybody saw our faces before?" Ben asked. "Besides, even if they think they recognize us, they wouldn't believe that we'd come back there so soon. I'm tellin' ya, this is foolproof."

"I'm with you, Ben," Belle said. "You just lead the way."

"That's another thing," Ben said. "Having a woman with us is gonna make us look different."

"Take it easy, Ted," Jake said. "It'll go down easy, just like Ben says."

Griff was the last to mount, painfully swinging his leg up over the saddle.

"You all right?" Ben asked.

"I'm fine," Griff said. "I'm just thinkin' maybe I shouldn't get off my horse."

"That's a good idea," Ben said. "Stay mounted and on watch. Belle . . ."

"I got the horses," she said.

"Right. Me, Jake, and Ted will go inside, and this time," he gave them a hard look, "*this* time we're gettin' that safe."

FORTY-FOUR

After being awakened by Sally's mouth nibbling on him, and then engulfing him, Clint and Sally both got up and went downstairs for breakfast. During breakfast, Carl Mason came in and joined them.

"Something to eat, Carl?"

"No," Mason said, "can't eat. I'm nervous."

"About what, Carl?" asked Sally.

Mason looked at Clint, who imperceptibly shook his head.

"Just bein' the actin' sheriff and all, Miss Sally," Mason finally said.

"Oh, Carl, you'll do a fine job."

"I hope so."

She finished her coffee and said, "I have to get to work. I'll see you later?" she asked Clint.

"You bet."

As she got up and left, bidding the sheriff good day,

165

Mason seemed to realize who it was for the first time, and what it meant that she was here.

"Did you two—"

"We did."

"Well, I'll be damned," Mason said. "I never would have thought it of her."

"What? That she'd have sex, or with me?"

"Neither," he said. "I just thought that one would take a heap of courtin'."

"And she might," Clint said, "but I'm not courtin', Carl."

Mason still shook his head and said, "I'll be damned."

"Did you find us any help?"

That had been one of the things they'd discussed before Clint left the jail last night, the possibility of some of the townspeople taking up guns and helping out.

"Nope. Not after what happened to the last posse."

"That's not a surprise."

When Clint had been a town sheriff he discovered how people take you for granted and assume that you're going to solve every problem yourself, without any help. It just didn't work that way.

"So it's you and me," Clint said.

"I guess."

"Have some coffee," Clint said.

"Shouldn't we be gettin' over to the bank?" Mason asked.

"If we go over there, the Bortons will see us," Clint said. "What we want them to do is go into the bank."

"How will we know when they're in?"

"They can't go in until it opens, and it doesn't open

for half an hour. We've got time. We'll take some chairs outside and sit so we can see the front of the bank. At the first sign of trouble, we'll move.''

"What's the first sign of trouble?"

"Don't worry, Carl," Clint said, "I'll know it when I see it.''

When they came within sight of the town, Ben held up his hand to stop the small convoy.

"Okay," he said, "Jake and I are gonna go first. Ted, you come in after us. Belle and Griff, bring up the rear. We ain't goin' into the bank until it opens. Got it?''

They all said they did.

"Griff?''

"Yeah, Ben?''

"Don't shoot no women this time.''

"I won't," Griff said, and then added under his breath, "as long as no woman gets in my way.''

"Okay, then," Ben Borton said, "let's get this over with.''

FORTY-FIVE

Clint and Mason were seated in their chairs when the first two robbers made their appearance.

"How can you tell?" Mason asked. "Maybe they're just a couple of sodbusters come to town for a cold beer."

"Most sodbusters, or ranch hands, or anybody coming in off the trail, don't get in this early," Clint said. "They camp somewhere, then wake up, have some coffee, and start moving again. These two would have had to be camped just outside of town to ride in now. If they were that close, why didn't they come in and get hotel rooms?"

"So you're guessing?"

"I'm not guessing," Clint said. "Look at them, for Chrissake. Their shoulders are tense and they're looking all around them. They're waiting to see if anyone is going to recognize them."

"Okay, so it's them," Mason said, nervously. "Do we move now?"

"No," Clint said, "we want the whole gang."

"But the odds are even, now," Mason said. "Two on two. If we wait, we'll be outnumbered."

"That may be," Clint said, "but we have the element of surprise on our side. They don't know that we've been expecting them."

"I can't believe they came in today," Mason said. "I thought we'd have to wait for days."

"I guess it's a good thing I thought of it when I did," Clint said. "We could have left town and missed it all while searching for them out there."

"So it's a coincidence?"

Clint made a face and said, "I guess."

The two riders reined in their horses in front of the bank and then made like they were waiting for it to open. A third rider came in while they were waiting and did the same thing. He tied off his horse and tried to look impatient. When the fourth and fifth riders came, it was all the proof Clint needed that this was the gang.

"I know that woman," he said. "Her name's Belle, and she's with the gang."

"Where's the fifth brother?" Mason asked.

"He's probably wounded," Clint said, "and can't make it. We'll have to go and get him later."

"So what do we do now?"

"We wait for some of them to go inside, and then we take the ones who are outside."

"Won't the ones inside hear us?"

Clint smiled at Mason and said, "We'll do it quietly."

He got out of his chair. "Come with me. This is what we're going to do . . ."

When Belle and Griff rode into town, Ben said to Jake and Ted, "Should be opening soon."

As he said it they heard the lock on the bank door snick open and then the door itself opened. For a moment, Ben was startled. He thought it was the same bank manager, but then realized it was the brother, the head teller.

"Come right in, gentlemen," the man said. "The bank is open for business."

"Much obliged," Ben said, and he and Jake walked past the man without being recognized. Ted nodded to the man and entered behind them.

Once the three men were inside, Clint and Mason made their move . . .

"I can't walk right up to them," Clint had told him earlier, "because the woman will recognize me. You'll have to distract them."

"How?"

"Just stumble up to them like you're drunk—and take off that badge."

Griff saw the man first from astride his horse, and then Belle spotted him.

"Drunk comin'," she said.

Mason was weaving back and forth, singing under his breath. He had one hand at his side and the other behind his back.

"What do we do?" Belle asked.

"Leave him be," Griff said. "He's no danger to any-one."

Griff was more concerned with his wound. Inside his pants he could feel that the ride into town had started him bleeding again. Blood was dripping down his leg and would soon drip out onto his boot and then the ground. He wondered if he'd get some kind of infection and maybe have to have his leg cut off.

While Griff was worrying about his leg, Clint worked his way up the alley next to the bank. When he peeked out, he could see Griff on his horse, but he couldn't see Belle or Mason. He was going to have to be extra quick.

Mason continued to weave and sing, and then lifted his head and looked right at Belle.

"Pretty lady," he said, aloud. "Hey, pretty lady? Wan' have a drink with me?"

"Go away, Mister," Belle said. "If you know what's good for you, go away."

Belle was wearing a holster—Will's holster—and she came awful damn close to drawing her gun to scare the drunk away.

"He just wants to take you for a drink, Belle," Griff said.

"I don't drink with drunks."

That didn't stop Mason. He needed to get a little closer, so he kept coming.

"Get away from me!" Belle yelled, and started to go for her gun.

"Don't!" Mason said. He dropped his drunk guise and brought his hand out from behind his back, where he'd been holding his gun. "Don't try it."

Belle froze. It took precious seconds for Griff to pull

his attention away from the blood that was staining his pants and his boots, and by that time Clint had come out of the alley.

"Don't be foolish," he called to Griff.

Griff turned and saw Clint covering him.

"Who are you?"

"The man who's going to put you away, Borton," Clint said. "You and your brothers."

"You're Adams," Griff said, "Clint Adams."

"That's right. Now drop your gun."

Griff's eyes darted around.

"I said drop it."

"Okay, okay."

"Left hand."

Griff reached across his body and withdrew his pistol from his holster with his left hand. He bent over like he was going to drop it—and then he threw it right through the bank window, shattering the glass.

FORTY-SIX

Inside the bank, Ben Borton had just made their presence and purpose known to the tellers and the bank manager.

"Oh, God," Sam Gateway said, "it's you . . . again?"

"Yes, again," Ben said, covering him.

All Sally could think of was that she was glad the man who had terrorized her was not with them. These men didn't seem concerned with her.

"All right, Mr. Manager," Ben said. "I guess you got the job after the last robbery, huh? Got your brother fired?"

"He wasn't fired," one of the male tellers said. "You killed him."

"You got the wrong man, fella," Ben said. "I remember shooting a man, all right, but it wasn't the bank manager. Why would I shoot the only person who could open the safe?" He looked directly at Sam Gateway and added, "Which is what you're gonna do right now."

173

"I can—" Gateway started to say, but he was interrupted by something shattering the front window of the bank.

"What the hell—" Ben said.

"Gun!" Ted yelled, looking at the object on the floor. The grips were pearl-handled. "Griff's gun."

"Check outside!" Ben said.

Ted went to the door and looked outside.

"Shit," he said. "Shit, shit, shit! I don't see Belle or Griff."

"Goddamn them," Ben said, "they got taken."

"By who?" Jake asked.

"That's what we got to find out," Ben said. He turned to the bank manager. "Mister, you better get that safe open."

"Opening the safe won't do you any good," Sam Gateway said.

"And why not?"

"Because there's no money in it."

"Sure there ain't."

"It's true," Gateway said. "We moved the money last night, emptying the safe."

Ben stared at the man and knew instinctively that he was telling the truth.

"Now," he said, "why would you want to go and do that?"

"Whatta we do now?" Jake asked.

"You said 'we' moved the money, old man," Ben said. "Who's we?"

"The deputy and Clint Adams."

Ben looked at Jake and said, "Well, I guess that answers the question of who's out there."

"It still doesn't answer my question," Jake said. "What do we do now?"

"We got hostages," Ben said. "We take them out of here with us."

"What about Griff and Belle?"

"We'll have to come back for them. Come on, you each take a teller, I'll take the manager."

"Why do you have to take me?" Gateway complained. "There are three of you, and three tellers."

"What's the matter, old man, scared?"

"Don't take me," Sam Gateway said, pointing at Sally Olson, "take her."

Sally stared at Gateway as if he was some sort of insect.

"Oh, we are taking her, Mr. Manager," Ben said, "but we're taking you, too." He looked at his brothers and said, "Let's go. We're gettin' out of here."

Clint covered the front of the bank while Mason took Griff and Belle right across the street to the jail. He came running back in moments.

"They're locked in next to the money," he said. "What did I miss?"

"Not a thing," Clint said. "Nothing's happened since the gun went through the window."

"What do you think they'll do?"

"I know what they'll do," Clint said. "They'll come out with hostages."

"We'll have to let them go, then," Mason said, "or they'll kill the hostages."

"If we let them go, Carl, they'll kill them anyway, once they get far enough away from town. Except for

Sally. They might keep her alive, for a while.''

"So what do we do?"

"Keep them covered when they come out," Clint said, "and wait for a shot. Right now, though, let's get their horses away from the bank."

"Damn it!" Ted said, still looking out the front.

"What is it?" Ben asked.

"They took our horses."

"Don't worry," Ben said. "We'll get them back. Jake, you take the girl."

"Got her," Jake said, moving toward Sally.

"Ted, take one of the other tellers."

"What do we do with the third one?"

"Put him down, but don't kill him."

Ted walked over to where the two tellers were standing, one young, one old, both frightened.

"Which one wants to go?"

"Take me," the older man said. "He's too young."

Ted drew his gun and raised it to hit the older man.

"No, don't hit him," the young teller said. "He won't be able to take it. Hit me."

Ted stared at the boy, then brought the gun down on the older man.

"He'd only slow us down," he said to the young teller. "Come here." He pulled the teller against him, so he could use him as a shield. Jake was doing the same thing with Sally, holding her in front of him.

"Come on, Mr. Manager," Ben said, grabbing Sam Gateway, "time to go."

FORTY-SEVEN

"You want me to what?" Carl Mason asked in disbelief.

"If you see a shot," Clint said, again, "take it. Don't hesitate."

"But . . . they'll have hostages in front of them," the acting sheriff argued.

"Carl," Clint said, "if we let them ride out of here with those people, they're as good as dead."

"But . . . what if I miss?"

"You know all those bottles and cans you've been shooting at?"

"Yeah?"

"Was all that practice for nothing?"

"Well, no . . ."

"Then don't miss."

"Jesus, I don't know—"

"Here they come."

Suddenly, Carl Mason's palms were soaking wet.

Ben came out first, with Sam Gateway in front of him.

After that, Jake came out with Sally, and Clint's heart sank. The third brother came out with a young male teller.

"Who's in charge?" Ben yelled.

"Answer him," Clint said.

He and Mason had taken cover across the street, in front of the hardware store, which wasn't open yet.

"I am," Mason said. "I'm Sheriff Mason."

"I thought you was all shot up?" Ben called back.

"I'm the acting sheriff," Mason replied. "You did shoot the sheriff, but he's gonna be all right."

"Well, I'm glad to hear that," Ben said, sounding like a very amiable fellow. "Why don't you stand up so we can see what an acting sheriff looks like."

Mason didn't have to be told that that was a bad idea.

"Okay, never mind," Ben said. "I'm sure you can see we got some company here."

"I see it."

"Is Clint Adams with you?"

Mason looked at Clint, who nodded for him to answer the question.

"Yes, he's here."

"Sing out, Adams!"

"I'm here, Borton. Let those people go. Hiding behind them is not going to do you any good."

"You don't think so? You don't think I'd kill this man if you don't do as I say?"

"You want your horses, right?" Clint asked.

"That's right."

"And I suppose you want Belle and your brother, too?"

"Hey, that would be nice."

"None of that is going to happen."

"Well, if it doesn't, say good-bye to these good people," Ben said.

"Ben—it is Ben, isn't it?"

"That's right."

"You have a reputation for being smart," Clint said. "We can't let you leave here with those hostages. You know that. As soon as you got away you'd kill them."

"You won't take my word that we won't?"

"Sorry."

"Then I guess we'll just have to shoot them here and take our chances."

"You shoot them and you're dead."

Finally, Ben Borton made the gesture Clint had been waiting for. He was about to say something, and he gestured with his gun hand, moving it away from his body just far enough.

Clint fired, and the bullet hit Ben Borton and shattered his forearm. He screamed, and his gun went flying. He released Gateway, who turned and tried to run back into the bank. Accidentally, he ran right into Sally and Jake, making them stagger back and giving Mason his shot. He fired and his bullet struck Jake in the chest, missing his heart by inches, but hitting his lungs. He fell to the ground, clutching his chest, and would soon drown in his own blood.

"Don't shoot!" Ted Borton yelled. He released his hostage and held his hands in the air. "Don't shoot."

Clint looked at Mason and said, "Good shot."

When the street was cleaned up of Bortons, a bandaged Ben and disgraced Ted were in a cell next to Griff and

Belle. In the third cell sat the money, which Ben Borton could only look at. Clint and Mason had one more thing to take care of before they rode out and brought in the last brother. Ted had told them where to look.

Clint and Mason entered the bank, where the employees were gathered around the older man who had been knocked out.

"I'm all right," he insisted.

The young teller looked up at Clint and Mason and said, "That was some shootin'!"

"Thanks," Clint said. "That's what the sheriff here gets paid for. Where's Mr. Gateway, Sally?"

"In his office, hiding, I think."

Clint and Mason went to the bank manager's door and entered without knocking. Gateway was behind his desk, holding a glass in one hand and a bottle of whiskey in the other.

"Not so easy, is it, Gateway?" Clint asked.

"W-what?"

"Being manager of a bank," Clint went on. "It's not so easy."

Gateway scowled and didn't say anything.

"Where's your gun, Gateway?" Clint asked.

Gateway sat back and removed the gun from his shoulder holster. Clint walked over to him and snatched it away from him.

"A man who is afraid to use guns shouldn't be carrying one—except you weren't afraid to use it on your own brother, were you?"

"W-wha—"

"During the robbery you saw a chance to become bank manager. When the robbers fired their shots, you took out your gun and fired it once, into the head of your brother."

"I didn't—"

"I can smell that this gun has been fired, Gateway. You didn't bother to clean it after you used it. You killed your brother, all right. Nobody saw anyone pull the trigger, and the Borton Boys swear they didn't do it."

"And you believe them?" Gateway asked.

"I do," Clint said. "Do you know why?"

"Why?" the man asked, glumly.

"Because I have more respect for them than I do for you."

Gateway turned his head so that he wasn't looking at either man.

"I didn't mean it," he said. "It just happened—sort of spur of the moment."

Clint handed Mason the man's gun and said, "He's all yours, Sheriff."

J. R. ROBERTS
THE GUNSMITH

Explore the exciting Old West with one of the men who made it wild!